CYCLING THROUGH EDEN

A Novel

By

Edward L. Kottick

This book is a work of fiction. Places, events, and situations in this story are purely fictional. Any resemblance to actual events or persons, living or dead, is purely coincidental.

Cover art by Andrew Schiller.

Book Hatchery, LLC, Cedar Falls, Iowa
www.bookhatchery.com

To Gloria, my loving wife, who knew before I did that I had a novel in me, and whose support I cherish; and to Andrew Schiller, my grandson, my cycling companion, and the outstanding graphic artist responsible for the cover of this book.

CHAPTER ONE

"And the Lord God planted a garden in Eden, in the east, and there he put the man whom he had formed." (Genesis 4:8)

Tendrils of wispy pink clouds creep across the pristine sky, harbingers of the light that will drive away the darkness. A fiery orb climbs the eastern horizon, a nuclear furnace of ferocious intensity, every second converting seven million tons of hydrogen to helium with an explosive energy of heat and light that spews from its surface at speeds up to 15,000 miles per hour. All existence on Earth owes its survival to these life-giving rays; hence, it is provident that a small yet sufficient amount reaches this new world with its pristine Garden.

Bathed in the beneficent light and warmth of its star, the Garden begins to come alive. A riot of reds, yellows, blues, and purples spreads through the luxurious verdant foliage, as a rich carpet of phlox, carnations, firelace, lilies, and death blossoms unfold their petals in response to the refulgent sunlight. Graceful gazelles, long-necked giraffes, striped zebras, and bearded wildebeests stroll unafraid past fierce tigers, majestic lions, spotted cheetahs, and sleek leopards. They are joined by smaller mammals—foxes, raccoons, marmosets, jackals, sloths, and mongooses—while playful monkeys, chimpanzees, lemurs, and gibbons swing through branches overhead. Marsupials with laden pouches explore the underbrush. Colorful macaws, toucans, parrots, and kingbirds populate the acacia, manzanello, walnut, ginkgo, and baobab trees. Great birds of paradise hang from above, while beneath, strutting peacocks spread their vibrant plumage. Gila monsters, frogs, pythons, boa constrictors, geckos, chameleons, and tortoises slither along the ground. The waters are filled with swordfish, sharks, goldfish, guppies, lampreys, eels, mollusks, and crustaceans in never-ending profusion. On land the air is animated with sound, from the lusty trumpeting of elephants to the deep-throated roars of tigers, from the barking of jackals to the neighing of zebras, from the cries of macaws and the cacophony of the song birds to the grunting

1

chatter of the primates, all in counterpoint to the insistent buzzing drone of the flourishing insect population.

The lion stirs, awakened by the day. He is a king among beasts, with a body of coiled muscle weighing nearly 500 pounds. His tawny coat is set off by a luxurious dark brown mane. The muscles in his powerful shoulders and large chest ripple like crinkled gold in the sunlight. He plants his massive paws in front of him and stretches to his full eight-foot length. He yawns, baring his sharp claws and long incisors, driving away the cobwebs of nothingness. He hears something—a distant rhythmic whirring—more a sensation than a sound. His sharp yellow eyes search the landscape, but he sees nothing untoward. He crouches down to wait for the disturbance to materialize, but is soon distracted by the fragrant air, with its rich, invigorating oxygen content and its aromatic jungle smells. The lion sniffs, his nose quivering uncontrollably, his keen senses nearly overwhelmed by the perfume of the Garden. He rolls onto his back, his legs in the air, like a kitten with catnip, intoxicated by the rich odors.

But soon his stomach growls. He senses a void within. He notices a meaty-looking substance before him, something not there a moment ago. He sniffs; it fills his nostrils with joy. He recognizes it as sustenance and eats majestically, filling his empty belly with the life-giving matter. He drinks deeply from a nearby stream of crystal-clear water, refreshing himself with the cool, clean liquid he conveys to his mouth with his tongue. Purring with contentment, he settles back, his attention once more drawn to the now insistent whirring. The hum grows more audible, like an invading army of insects, and his abdomen feels the ground vibrate with its approach. He begins to make out the source of the disturbance, approaching rapidly from his right, on a smooth, five-foot-wide ribbon of macadam that curves through the Garden. The object sweeps by him: a tandem bicycle propelled by two figures, diligently hunched over the drops of their handlebars. The lion watches as it swiftly disappears on his left. His curiosity has been satisfied. He is no longer interested. Right now a nap is more important. The Garden quiets as the inhabitants settle down, their stomachs filled with food and water that—like the lion's—

materialized to assuage their hunger.

Although they have been at it since shortly after first light, the occupants of the tandem do not stop to rest. The cyclists do not appear to be working hard, nor are they perspiring, although they are traveling at a speed of 25 miles per hour. The macadam they ride on slopes at a two percent downgrade. The ambient temperature of the air is a pleasant 72 degrees Fahrenheit, and the relative humidity is 40 percent. With a 10-mile-per-hour wind at their backs, with their legs spinning like well-oiled pistons in a pedaling cadence of 80 revolutions per minute, with their chain fixed in a 100 gear, with the wheels of their self-propelled vehicle thrumming monotonously on the macadam, Adam and Eve are circumnavigating Eden.

Their tandem is an old Schwinn, its chromium-molybdenum frame painted a dull red and its shift levers mounted on the captain's down tube. It is a simple 10-speed machine, with a 39/52 chain ring and a 28/24/20/17/14 rear cluster. Its inch-and-a-quarter tires, filled to the recommended pressure of 90 pounds per square inch, never need refilling. Its chain never needs lubricating. It is capable of 10 changes of gear, but only the highest is in use; in fact, neither Adam nor Eve would know how to shift a gear had they been required to do so. And although it will not be developed in this form before the early twentieth century, the manner of their transportation is simply an indication that the laws of time and space are as yet foreign to Eden. The presence of the macadam path is another indication that these laws have not yet been established; but long after they hold sway, the paths of the macadamized road and the bicycle will intersect. As so often happens, the result will follow the law of unintended consequences.

The cyclists' vision is limited to the fringes of the macadam, as if they were wearing blinders. The sights, sounds, and smells of the Garden are of no interest to them, and Adam's attention is fixed unswervedly on the road ahead. This is his task: to keep his machine centered on the macadam and to maintain a speed of 25 miles per hour. With the smooth, downward-sloping roadbed, the consistent cadence of 80 revolutions per minute, the 100 gear, and the 10-mile-per-hour wind at their backs, the pace is not difficult to sustain and the couple's tempo is unvarying. This is what they have been made to do.

The motion of Eve's legs matches Adam's precisely, demonstrating the immutable law of the tandem: the captain and the stoker are locked in cadence. Unlike Adam, Eve is not preoccupied by the need to keep the tandem centered on the macadam, nevertheless, the kaleidoscopic view of the flora and fauna that line both sides of the path do not claim her attention either. Instead, her gaze is fixed on Adam's muscular back, his well-formed trapeziums, rhomboids, and deltoids, as he hunches over the drops of his handlebars.

When the fiery orb is directly overhead the tandem slows to a halt. Responding to some inner command, Adam applies his hand brakes. He and Eve simultaneously rotate their right pedals to their bottom positions. Both riders plant their left feet on the path just before they halt. Their right feet contact the ground when the bicycle comes to a complete stop, and two right legs simultaneously swing over the top tube. It is a classic tandem dismount. The cyclists lean their machine against a tree and walk a few steps to a nearby sylvan glade.

They are naked as jay birds. Adam is a handsome young man, six feet in height, broad-shouldered, with mocha-shaded skin and a well-formed, tightly-muscled body. His head is crowned with a halo of dark, curly hair. He is smooth-shaven, and will remain so as long as he is in Eden. His generous nose sits between wide-set grey eyes and over a firm mouth. His stomach is flat, his abdominals rock-like. His flaccid phallus peeks forth from a luxurious growth of pubic hair. His arms are powerful, his hands exude strength. His legs are long, with the prominent quadriceps of a professional athlete. Eve is a soft, lovely young woman, with a narrow waist, wide hips, a rounded bottom, and slender, shapely legs. A tightly-curled bush conceals her pudenda. Her small, globular breasts, with their prominent nipples, stand erect. The top of her head just reaches Adam's shoulder. Her unblemished skin and thick, wavy, shoulder-length hair are somewhat lighter than his, and her nose is smaller and straighter. Her

4

brown eyes look out at the world with the innocence of a new-born infant, and the corners of her full lips break upward, revealing perfect white teeth. Although newly created, Adam and Eve are teenagers, well past puberty, with fully-developed, vital bodies. They will retain this ageless youth as long as they remain in Eden.

The couple seat themselves on the ground. Manna appears before them, in the form of four small, soft, round, white cakes, each supplying one-sixth of their daily nutritional requirements. They consume two cakes each, conveying the bland, flaky substance to their mouths with their fingers. A nearby stream provides cool, refreshing water, which they drink lying on their stomachs, conveying the liquid to their lips with cupped hands. They rest, ignoring each other's presence. Wordlessly, they rise and return to the tandem. Adam places the machine on the macadam. Right legs over the top tube, they straddle the frame; left feet on pedals, they push off and seat themselves on their saddles. It is a classic tandem start.

Adam and Eve continue their ride. The grade of the macadam strip is always two percent; it is always down hill. They are always in their 100 gear. The 10-mile-an-hour wind is always at their backs. Their entire circumnavigation of the Garden will be achieved under these conditions. Like the laws of time and space, the laws of physics and mechanics have not yet been established.

When the sun is low on the western horizon the cyclists halt again, now returned to the point from which they had started early that morning. Once again, they find cakes of manna and a stream of cool, refreshing water close to hand. Adam and Eve have been bicycling all day and have covered 200 miles. Eons later, recreational cyclists will train for months to ride a "century"—a day's outing of 100 miles. It will be an organized event, for which participants will fill out registration forms and pay entrance fees. It will have rest stations every 25 miles or so, with portable toilets available, and with food and beverages laid out for the benefit of the riders. Vehicles will patrol the route, picking up stragglers. It will be considered an achievement to complete a century, and the cyclists who do so will receive t-shirts, pins, patches, and certificates attesting to their athletic prowess. Adam and Eve did a double century today, in eight hours of riding, and neither feels fatigue. As darkness falls they stretch out on the soft grass and immediately fall into dreamless sleep.

The next day in the Garden of Eden passes in much the same way as the first. The lion rises with the rosy-fingered dawn, eats his morning meal, and settles down to see if the tandem will pass again. What else does he have to do? He does not have to hunt; sustenance is provided for him, as it is for all the denizens of this wondrous Garden. His sharp claws and huge incisors are capable of ripping prey to shreds, but there is no prey. He does not even know what prey is. In fact, none of the animals need to hunt or seek food. Insects need not eat plant life; birds need not eat berries and fruit; no living creature, no flora or fauna, has a natural enemy. All is provided for them in this delightful environment, this splendid Garden. So the lion waits, and is soon rewarded: Adam and Eve pass by on their tandem at 25 miles per hour, pedaling at a cadence of 80 revolutions per minute in their 100 gear. As it was yesterday, and as it will be tomorrow, Adam's attention is focused on the macadam. Eve's attention is focused on Adam's back.

Time passes, each day the same as the last, although every seventh day Adam and Eve do not ride the tandem; instead they laze about, watching the animals watch them. They watch each other as well, each recognizing the other as a creature, just as the lion they see every morning is a creature. They do not realize that they are of the same species; in fact, they do not know anything about species. They see every living thing as an individual being, apart from other individual beings. For Adam there is the lion, there is the elephant, and there is the Eve, although none of these entities have names in Adam's mind. They are simply recognitions. For Eve there is the giraffe, the monkey, and the Adam. They do not talk to the lion, the elephant, the giraffe, or the monkey, and they do not talk to each other. At any rate, their powers of speech have yet to be discovered. They eat together, but apart. They sleep together, but apart. They eliminate bodily wastes with as much concern for privacy as the lion. They do not share any activity other than riding the tandem. Except for turning their pedals in a forced unison, they do not communicate with each other in any way. So goeth the days in Eden. Life is easy; life is good. Life is also goddamn boring.

CHAPTER TWO

I pick up a thick envelope from an architect's office in Murray Hill on 32nd and 3rd, take a swig from my water bottle, unlock my bike, sling my chain around my neck, mount up, and head cross-town on 34th Street. The light package I stuffed in my shoulder bag contains documents of some sort—what, I don't know, and I don't care. All I care about is steering through four choked lanes of cross-town traffic on this hot July day without getting killed. The delivery goes to one of the convention offices in the Javits Center on 34th and 11th and my dispatcher says it has to be there by noon. I can do that distance in 20 minutes when traffic is light, but this is 11:05 on a weekday morning, and traffic is not light. Cross streets like Park Avenue and The Avenue of Americas (or 6th Avenue, which is what it used to be) are the worst. The lights last forever and the traffic is so heavy there's no chance of cutting through on a red. A good cyclist can move a hell of a lot faster than a car in this heavy traffic, but there's a limit to what I can do today.

I started my shift at 8:00 this morning and I'm beginning to feel the effects of three hours in the saddle. I tend to ride in high gears, torquing the pedals, so I can make some time when the coast is clear, or when I see an opening in traffic; but high gears put an unholy strain on my knees, and they stress the drive train, too. My chain gets so stretched out from the tension that it needs to be replaced every six months. But I can't replace my knees. Some days they ache so bad by the time I get home that I pop five aspirin before dinner. Fortunately I'm young and I recover quickly, and by the next morning I'm ready to go again.

Right now my knees are OK, but my quads are starting to feel the strain. My back is getting sore from hunching over the drops. My arms ache from holding the bike steady through one pothole after another. My neck hurts from keeping my head up. My eyes sting from the sweat running down from under my helmet. My nasal passages are beginning to burn from inhaling traffic fumes. My butt is sore on general principles. The tension from threading my bike through the heavy traffic is starting to get to me. The noise of the cars, buses, trucks, horns, and sirens, the shouts of workers, and the hum of construction machinery blend into a familiar mind-numbing cacophony that bounces off the walls of the concrete canyons that line the streets. But that's how it is every morning around this time. I'll get through the day. I always do.

Just past 8th Avenue I nearly get doored. A parked Volvo opens on the driver's side, right into my path. I catch a quick glimpse of the driver as he steps out, a man in his 30s, wearing a jacket and tie in the heat. He sees me bearing down on him and he's frozen behind the door, a baffled rictus etched on his face. I clamp down on my brake levers as I twist my handlebars, and barely manage to get around him. That puts me in the path of a Ford van just behind me in the left-hand lane, but the Ford sees my maneuver, hits his brakes, and avoids hitting me by inches. I go around the Volvo and weave back into the inside lane, waving at the Ford in thanks. My heart is pounding from the adrenalin coursing through my body. In one split second I twice missed getting injured, or worse. Today must be my lucky day—yeah—some luck! I scream silently at the driver of the Volvo. I would love to have directed my ire verbally and loudly at that stupid son of a bitch, but I keep my temper on a leash.

It doesn't pay to rile up the civilians when they're behind the wheels of their 3,000-pound vehicles. They outweigh you and they can outrun you. If you get them mad enough they'll hunt you down, run you off the road, or squeeze you to the curb or against a parked car. The only advantage you have is your quickness and your clarity of mind, and you'll lose them both if you give way to anger. It didn't take me long to figure that out when I became a bike messenger. So I don't look back, and I resist the urge to hold up my middle finger. "Shit happens, Adam," I tell myself; "be professional." Of course, some of the guys would take revenge, going around the block and taking out one of the car's outside mirrors with their chain or lock. Like a lot of the messengers I wear my chain and lock around my neck, in an old inner tube. It would be pretty easy to swing that chain and bash in that shit-head's driver's mirror. Henny Muller does it all the time—he's famous for it. So far his lock has destroyed something like 15 side mirrors on cars and small trucks; in fact, he pastes a little smiley-face decal on his down tube every time he succeeds in destroyed an "enemy" mirror, like a World-War II fighter pilot painting a symbol on the side of his plane for every enemy he shoots down. I don't do it. "Be professional, Adam!" I keep telling myself. But someday one of those shit-heads is gonna push me too far.

Getting "doored," or getting a "door prize," as some of the guys called it, is the number one occupational hazard for a bike messenger. Jerry Messman got doored just last week, riding fast down 57th, when a woman opened a cab door on the wrong side. Jerry got his collarbone broken and he'll be out of action for weeks; but he was lucky. Eddie Ostlund collected a door prize on Madison last year, again someone getting out of a cab on the wrong side. Eddie went flying through the air, and when he came down he was plowed under by a Ford panel truck. The poor son of a bitch driving the truck was standing on his brakes, but the way things went, Eddie didn't stand a chance. He was killed immediately. We wore black armbands for a week, but it didn't bring Eddie back.

Almost everyone in this business collects a door prize if he's in it long enough. It hasn't happened to me yet, but I've had some close calls, like the one today. Fortunately, both Jerry and I work for an outfit that hires us as employees rather than independent contractors. The independents don't have taxes taken out of their pay, but if they step into some shit with their health it's on their shoulders; there's no insurance. Eddie was an independent. A lot of good his few extra bucks of take-home pay did him. Maybe it paid for his funeral.

It's one of those killer New York days, hot and muggy; but that doesn't stop the motorists from trying to get you. New York drivers hate bike messengers. In a way, I suppose you can't blame them. We appear out of nowhere, skittering across their paths like runaway horses. We come off sidewalks suddenly, as if we can't decide whether we're pede-strians or vehicles. We go up one-way streets, on sidewalks, on grass, through parks, through red lights, and zip past them on either side as they sit stalled in traffic. We fly through those streets like gazelles, while they lumber along like hippos. We're free to go where we want while they're chained to their air-conditioned mechanical beasts. They hate us for making their miserable lives even more miserable, and they hate us for our freedom.

Cab drivers are the worst. They despise bike messengers. They consider us the scum of the earth. Most of them would like to cut me off, or swerve into my lane, or block my progress, just for the fun of it. They do it every day, particularly when they don't have a fare. And if the cabbies aren't enough of a problem, their passengers are another. You're more likely to get doored by someone exiting a taxi than anyone else. Inattentive drivers are another hazard. When they just don't see you, you can never predict what they're going to do. Then there's the pedestrian who steps off the curb without checking to see what's coming. Now you have the choice of either knocking him down or swerving into the next lane and possibly getting hit by an oncoming car. The jay walkers are just as bad. They're so intent on getting across the street without getting creamed they often just don't see you. Generally speaking, as far as the civilians are concerned, you're the invisible man. Still, most fatalities happen when a bike meets one of the big boys—a bus, a truck, or an SUV. You learn to look at those vehicles with respect. They have their blind spots, and if you're smart you'll learn where they are and you'll stay out of them.

Biking isn't so dangerous if you're mooching along at five miles an hour, but a bike messenger has to move. I do 15 to 20 miles an hour and more when I can, much faster than the midtown traffic moves, because speed is what puts the bread on my table. Every package I deliver means a commission, and the more deliveries I make in a day the more money I go home with at the end of the week. I ride against one-way streets, through red lights, on sidewalks, through back yards, across lawns, over medians, and through private drives to deliver my packages as quickly as I can. I ride in weather so hot you could fry your eyeballs on the sidewalk. I ride in rainstorms so heavy you can't see three feet in front of you. I ride in weather so bone-chilling cold it takes half the night to get the feeling back into my toes. I'm 23 years old and I've been a bicycle messenger for two years, since I dropped out of NYU. There's a lot to be said for this job. I don't work in a cubicle, I don't write code or pound a keyboard all day, and I don't wear a suit and a tie. I'm in the fresh air—or at least, what passes for fresh air in this town—and no one breathes down my neck. I get to do what I love best, ride my bike. But it's a tough job and sometimes I wonder why I work so damned hard for a few lousy bucks. Yeah, I'm my own boss, and yeah, it's a free life; but it's not a good life, and I realize that every day, when I come home with my skin black with soot from exhaust fumes and road dirt.

Just before I reach 10th Avenue I hear a familiar and ominous sound behind me. I check the rear view mirror mounted on my helmet and see a yellow Humvee on my back wheel. The driver is some punk kid, pissed off at me because I'm in "his" lane. That I have as much right to the lane as he does makes no difference to him. That if he occupied my position there would still be a listless line of vehicles ahead of him still makes no difference to him. I have his lane, he's bigger than me, and that snot-faced kid is going to teach me a lesson by gunning his Humvee's engine, like he's going to run me down and make road kill out of me. I get one of those big, brave kids just about every day, driving a van, an SUV, or something else, as long as it's big. They think sitting in that left-hand seat makes them men. I stay in front of the Humvee for another block, just to annoy him, then stand on the pedals and peel off to the right on 11th, headed for Javits.

I reach the Javits Center at 11:49 and look for a rack or fence to chain my bike to. Of course, I don't find any—why should New York citizens be concerned about the safety of a messenger's vehicle? I have no choice, so I free-lock my machine, passing the chain through the front wheel and the frame. Anyone can pick up a free-locked bike and throw it into the back of a pickup, and I lost one that way in my first year on the job. Like most messengers, I deliberately make my bike look junky with some spray paint. Most people wouldn't recognize that it's a valuable aluminum-frame road bike, but bike thieves are onto that. But they also know that a messenger is never gone from his machine for very long, that messengers carry radios, and that messengers will hunt them down relentlessly. Mostly, they leave us alone.

The Javits Center is an enormous complex, but the office is on the first floor. I find it immediately and deliver my package to the woman behind the counter. It's a swanky air-conditioned setup and the receptionist is one hot babe. I'd like to chat her up and cool off a little, but she turns her attention back to her computer screen as soon as she signs my delivery form. I get the point: I'm a hot, dirty messenger, dressed in a sweaty Mets t-shirt, black biking shorts, and a grimy set of cycling gloves, and I have no place in her cool little climate-controlled tight-assed world. I place the signed form in the pocket of my shoulder bag as I leave the office; I'll need to turn that in to base at the end of my shift. It's the only proof I have that the package was delivered. The company gets upset when a delivery form is lost, and I lose my commission to boot, so I'm careful with those little slips of paper.

I'm back to my bike in less than four minutes. I pull the radio from the holster on the strap of my bag and call dispatch:

"Hey, Dottie, it's Double-Oh-Seven at Javits. Mission accomplished. What next?"

Dottie doesn't waste words with pleasantries: "Oh-Oh-Seven, Dr. Richard Clark, 976 3rd to Sinai mail." *("Pick up a package from Dr. Richard Clark at 976 3rd Avenue, and deliver it to the mail room at Mt. Sinai Hospital.")*

Shit. Mt. Sinai is uptown on 99th and Madison, and my territory is midtown. And I have to go all the way back across town, down to 3rd Street again, for the pickup. Dottie doesn't like me and I'm not sure if she's giving me this long ride just to screw me or because I'm the only messenger available. Either way there's no sense complaining, because my livelihood depends on keeping a good relationship with my dispatcher.

"OK, Dottie, Dr. Richard Clark, 976 3rd to Sinai mail. 10-4."

I grab a power bar out of my bag for lunch, take a swig from my water bottle, unlock my bike, mount up, and I'm off, out of the saddle, flying down 11th Avenue.

CHAPTER THREE

"And out of the ground the Lord God made to grow. . . the tree of the knowledge of good and evil." (Genesis 2:9)

God created the universe. God created mass and energy. God created the stars and the heavens and the sun and the moon. God created the galaxies, the dark matter, the black holes, the quasars, the planets, the planetoids, and the asteroids. He created comets, meteors, and meteorites. He created the earth and all its creatures, great and small. He created the animals, the birds, the insects, and the fish in the sea. He created vegetables and minerals. He created bacteria and viruses. He created the elements. He created molecules and atoms and electrons, and protons and neutrons, and gluons and quarks and leptons. He created gravity and the electromagnetic force and the strong and weak forces.

But God did not create an immutable universe.

Hence, Eve awakens one day to a sound never before heard in the Garden. It is speech. It comes from a snake, a handsome boa constrictor, lounging nearby, warming its body with the first rays of the morning sun.

"Good morning, Eve," he says politely, "I'm the snake. You probably don't realize it, but you and Adam are both mankind. He is man. You are woman. He is the same as you; you are the same as him." With that, the boa begins to glide away on its comically tiny legs.

Eve opens her mouth and speaks. "Wait," she cries out. "Explain what you mean."

Eve realizes—with great wonderment—that she heard speech; that she understands speech; that she herself is capable of speech; and that her name is Eve. It is a revelation. Eve has never experienced a revelation before; Eve has scarcely experienced anything before. Eve has gained knowledge, and it is a new thing for her. Eve is excited. Excitement is new, too.

The boa returns. He is a large, slender, fine-looking reptile, fully ten feet in length, with colorful brown, cream, and tan markings. His prehensile tail swishes back and forth nervously, and his forked tongue flickers rhythmically in and out from between his thin, grinning lips. His beady eyes fix on Eve.

"I mean that you and Adam belong to the same species. He is the male, you are the female. The differences between you are minor and of no consequence."

The snake seems in no hurry to leave, so Eve persists. "How could we belong to the same species? My hair is long and his is short."

The snake hisses in reply, "You could cut your hair; he could grow his longer."

"But he is taller and I am shorter."

"The male of the species is often bigger than the female," responds the boa.

"He is stronger than I am."

"The male of the species is often stronger than the female."

"I have breasts and he has none."

"In mammals the female of the species always has breasts and the male has none."

"He voids water through a penis growing from between his legs, while I void water through a vagina whose lips grow from between my legs."

"In mammals the male of the species always has a penis and the female always has a vagina," says the snake. With that, his forked tongue flicks out in farewell and he quickly slithers away into the underbrush.

Eve is overwhelmed with knowledge. She has learned that both she and the creature who captains her tandem are of the same species. She has learned that his name is Adam. She has learned that the other animals are also members of species, but other species. She has learned to understand the concept of species. She has learned that she has speech. She has learned that she can communicate. And, as she wonders why she didn't know these things before, she has also learned to question. Unfortunately, she has not learned enough to question the circular reasoning supplied by the boa constrictor.

Adam awakes shortly thereafter and finds an animated Eve hovering over him. Now Adam hears speech for the first time, and like Eve, he finds that he understands it. "Adam," he hears her say breathlessly, and he knows this is his name. "Adam, a snake was just here."

Adam grunts, trying to slow down the unfamiliar auditory onslaught.

"Snake," he repeats, astounded that he not only understands language but is able to use it himself, astounded that he is understanding something new, something other than tandem, macadam, ride, manna, water, elimination, and sleep.

"Yes, a big boa constrictor," says Eve excitedly, enjoying the very sensation of excitement. "The snake told me that you and I belong to the same species."

"Species," utters Adam, who is not adapting to speech as readily as the animated creature in front of him.

"Yes," continues Eve. "You and I belong to the same species. You are a male, I am a female. The differences between us are minor and of no consequence."

Adam is trying to take this in. "Differences," he says.

"Yes," she replies, "my hair is long and yours is short, but I could cut my hair and you could grow yours longer. You are taller, but the male of the species is often bigger than the female. You are stronger, but the male of the species is often stronger than the female. I have breasts and you have none, but in mammals the female of the species always has breasts and the male has none. You void water through a penis between your legs, while I void water through the lips of a vagina between my legs, but in mammals the male always has a penis and the female always has a vagina."

Adam is nonplused by this long speech. "Mammals," he repeats. "Penis. Vagina."

The outburst of communication over, Adam and Eve perform their morning eliminations as unselfconsciously as before; but speech has brought them a new awareness of each other's presence, while the primitive discussion of gender distinctions has provoked in each an interest in the other's anatomy. Adam observes that the creature who stokes his tandem is comely and vivacious, with a narrow waist, apple-like breasts, sparkling eyes, smiling lips, and even teeth. Eve notes Adam's striking physique, his broad shoulders, his muscular frame, his curly hair, and his flaring nostrils. But these observations are made with no more emotional association than one would see in a rock. They eat their manna in silence— simultaneously eating and conversing is not yet among their rapidly-growing skills; and since God has not given them much time for idle chit-chat, they soon find it time to mount their tandem. They pedal down the macadam path (two percent downgrade, a tail wind of 10 miles per hour, turning the pedals at 80 revolutions per minute, making a speed of 25 miles per hour in a 100 gear), their heads whirling with knowledge. They gingerly exercise their new-found powers of speech and find that they now know the names of things. Nouns are exhilarating.

"Tandem," announces Adam proudly, nodding his head to indicate the machine beneath them. "Macadam," he says, nodding his chin at the road ahead of him. "Handlebar; saddle; wheel; tire; chain; brake." With great pleasure Adam is exhausting his vocabulary of his immediate surroundings.

Eve takes over. "Back," she proclaims cheerfully, touching the skin she'd been staring at without comprehension since the beginning of creation. "Head, arms, legs, hands, feet," she continues merrily, systematically identifying Adam's visible body parts. Eve begins to look beyond their selves and their transportation. "Zebra," she shouts, and Adam, searching for the beast, takes his eyes off the macadam. That is a mistake. The front wheel begins to wobble and the bicycle swerves, almost leaving the path. The riders throw their bodies around wildly, trying to avoid a spill. More through luck than skill, Adam manages to return the vehicle to the center of the road. Shaken by the close call, he breaks out in a sweat. He has never sweated before. He realizes he has learned something new: *keep your eyes on the road!* He has also learned that knowledge can be gained from experience, and that knowledge can be dangerous. Eve is happy that her captain has retaken control of their vehicle, but her eyes know no restraint.

The lion watches the tandem glide by, puzzled by the sounds emanating from its riders. "Lion," he hears, and realizes that that is him. Knowledge has come to the lion as well as to Adam and Eve. The lion is puzzled by knowledge. His noble brow furrows momentarily, but it is not in his nature to ponder such things. Instead, he settles down for a nap.

"Elephant," cries Eve happily. "Walnut tree, carnation, monkey, mongoose, macaw, fox, tortoise, gazelle, tiger, baobab." They find that they recognize colors as well. "Red poppies," calls Eve. "Yellow dandelions. Brown lion. Blue sky. White clouds. Green leaves." Eve is indefatigable. Adam takes it all in, but he keeps his eyes on the road. Verbs are more of a challenge. "Riding," states Eve. "We are riding. Adam and Eve are riding. Adam and Eve ride the red tandem."

Adam joins in. "Turning. We are turning the pedals. The wheels of the red tandem are turning."

The tandem stops at noon, as usual. "Manna," offers Eve. "Stream, water."

"Eat," replies her companion. "We eat manna. We drink water from the stream."

After their rest the pair remount the tandem. The afternoon's ride is spent in comparative silence; Speech has tired them and besides, by now they have named everything in sight. They complete their circumnavigation, consume their manna, drink from the stream, and fall into deep sleep. Adam and Eve are exhausted from their first day of sentience.

They wake at first light, as usual. They are tired this morning, paying a price for the mental and verbal immoderation of the previous day. They mount the tandem after their breakfast manna and proceed to the day's ride. Neither finds it as easy to pedal at the indefatigable pace they have always maintained, so there is little talk; instead, they concentrate on putting forth the effort needed to pedal at their expected 25-mile-per-hour pace. They are not used to exertion, but they manage to finish the daily ride and return to their base without incident. They eat, lie down, and instantly fall asleep.

The sun is already high in the sky when they awake the next morning. This puzzles them, since they have no concept of time spent sleeping. For all they know, the sun has simply started its daily journey a little further along today. They cannot explain this, although they ask each other what it means. Fortunately, today is a day of rest. They need it; they are tired again this morning, this time from the previous day's effort to maintain their usual speed. As they glumly eat their manna the boa constrictor slithers out of the bush. His glittering diamond patterns look particularly splendid today.

"Well, you two look pretty beat this morning," he offers.

This is Adam's first glimpse of the reptile, but from Eve's description he knows exactly who he is.

"You're the snake, aren't you?" he asks.

"Yes indeed, Adam," replies the boa managing a mock bow. "Snake, at your service. But why are you so worn-out today?"

Eve answers his question. "Well, yesterday's ride took a lot of effort." Eve's powers of speech have improved dramatically in the last 24 hours.

"Effort?" repeats the snake, fixing a look of puzzlement on his face. "Why should that be? What gear were you using?"

Now Adam is puzzled. "Gear? What is a gear?"

"Look," says the snake, gliding toward their tandem on his stunted legs. "Do you see these little levers?" He points at the shifters on the down tube with his tail. "They're connected to your front and rear sprockets by these cables, and they control the gears. The one on the left manages the chain wheels, with its two sprockets. The one on the right operates the rear cluster, with its five sprockets. Put the two of them together and you have 10 gears."

Adam's head spins from the effort to understand the boa. He doesn't know left from right, much less gears, levers, sprockets, cables, and chain wheels. The snake's explanation gets more complex.

"Look Adam, you have 27-inch diameter wheels." Adam is lost already. "Check out the position of the chain—see which of the front and rear sprockets it's on. Then divide the number of teeth on that chain ring by the number of teeth on that rear cluster and multiply that by your 27-inch wheels. Right now your chain is on the 52-tooth sprocket in front and the 14-tooth sprocket in the rear. If you divide 52 by 14 and multiply that by 27 you get 100 plus a bit. So you're riding in a 100 gear."

Adam doesn't know how to respond. This is higher mathematics to him, and he's not even familiar with the lower variety.

"What is a 100 gear?" he finally asks.

"Why," hisses the boa, "that's the equivalent of a front wheel that's 100 inches in diameter." Sly snake—he knows there isn't a chance in the world that Adam will know what he's talking about, but he persists, blinding the poor fellow with his gear chatter.

"Look, Adam," he continues, "if you move this right lever down a bit you derail the chain from the 14-tooth sprocket in the rear cluster and it slips onto the 17-tooth sprocket. Divide that 17 into the 52-tooth front sprocket, multiply that by 27, and you'll get 82.59. Call it 83. You'll be in an 83 gear. That will make it easier to pedal."

Adam hears only that it will be easier to pedal. Anything that will make it easier to pedal sounds good to him, so he asks the snake to repeat his instructions. Then, with a final wave of his colorful tail, a quick farewell, and a nod of his pointed head, the boa constrictor disappears. Adam and Eve sit on the ground cross legged, facing each other, their hands in their laps. They converse, a skill still new to them.

"Did you understand what the snake just said?"

"No, did you?"

"No."

"Did you understand anything the snake said?"

"No, did you?"

"No."

"I don't understand why yesterday's ride was so difficult."

"Maybe it's because we were tired?

"Why were we tired?"

"I don't know."

"I don't understand."

"I don't understand either."

"Maybe tomorrow's ride in the 83 gear will be easier."

"That would be nice."

"Do you understand what an 83 gear is?"

"No.

"Neither do I. Do know what a 100 gear is?"

"No."

"Neither do I."

"What is a sprocket?"

"I don't know."

"Neither do I."

"The snake's talk made my head hurt."

"Mine too. Why do you suppose that is?"

"I don't know. My body feels tired."

"Mine too."

"The sun is overhead. It must be time to eat our midday manna."

"OK, let's eat."

They consume their manna cakes, then overcome by drowsiness, fall asleep. This is new, too; they have never napped before. They wake after a few hours to find the sun on the wane. They are confused by the unaccustomed loss of consciousness as well as the apparent displacement of the sun, but they ignore the mystery; their brains are still trying to make sense out of gears. They try more conversation:

"Do you like manna?"

"Yes. Do you?"

"Yes."

"The warm sun feels good."

"Yes, it does."

They are inventing the art of social dialogue and still have a long way to go.

The next morning, after they get the tandem underway, Adam moves his right shift lever down just as the snake suggested, and is astonished to sense the chain move underneath him as it travels from the 14-tooth sprocket to the 17-tooth with a firm *kerchunk*. Adam has shifted into his 83 gear, just as the boa had described. The couple find the pedaling easier and are duly amazed. But soon enough they find that they aren't covering as much ground: with a two-percent downgrade, a 10-mile-an-hour tail wind, and a cadence of 80 revolutions per minute, they cannot make 25 miles per hour in an 83 gear. They pick up the pace to 90 revolutions per minute. This doesn't require as much torque power, but they're not used to turning their legs that quickly and the effort is tiring. After a brief consultation they decide to return to the 100 gear, and Adam manages to reverse the process. Now they can move along at their usual pace, and since they just had a day of rest with a nap, they have no difficulty finishing the circumnavigation with their usual aplomb. They decide that knowing how to shift into an 83 gear is not a very useful piece of knowledge.

The boa appears again the next day. This is getting to be a habit.

"Good morning, kids," he greets them. "How did you make out in the 83 gear?"

"Not too good," replies Adam. "It was nice at first, but we couldn't make enough speed unless we pedaled faster, and that got tiring." Adam has come to understand the concept of fatigue. "That 83 gear isn't worth much," he adds.

Eve joins in. "In order to complete our ride we had to switch back to the 100 gear." Eve is proud of the way she is throwing around gear numbers.

"Well that's too bad," hisses the snake. "But you know what will help?"

"No," they reply in chorus.

"Toe clips."

"Toe clips? What are toe clips?"

"Ah," hisses the pleased serpent, "toe clips are wonderful devices that attach to your pedals and strap around the toes of your feet. That way you can lift up on the pedal with one foot while the other foot is pushing its pedal down. That will give you more power in all your gears."

Adam and Eve ponder this new information. Life is getting complicated, but more power sounds good.

"How do we get these toe clips?" asks Eve, as Adam nods in agreement.

"Oh, I guess I can get a couple of pairs for you," says the boa, his forked tongue flicking in and out in anticipation. "Just give me a few days."

The serpent reappears on the next day of rest, after the midday meal. A small tool kit is strapped to his back and he is dragging two brand-new pairs of Binda Prestige nylon toe clips, one medium and one large, the white leather straps clamped between his teeth. He drops the pedaling aids at the feet of Adam and Eve, who examine them with unrestrained curiosity. They are things of beauty.

"OK kids," announces the reptile, "here they are. I'll tell you how to get them attached to your pedals."

Under the boa's direction Adam and Eve open the tool kit and remove a small box wrench and a screwdriver. They are not dexterous with hand tools, but with the reptile's coaching they manage to attach the toe clips to the platform pedals, the larger pair to the captain's, the smaller set to the stoker's.

"There!" says the boa. "You put your toes in here until they reach the front of the clips. Then you tighten these straps around the middle part of your feet. Now you'll be able to lift up on the pedals as well as push down. That will give you more power."

The pair return the wrench and screwdriver to the tool kit. The serpent's sly face is contorted with the effort to hide his satisfaction. "Enjoy," he hisses, as his silly little feet take him back into the jungle.

Our cyclists can't wait to start the ride the next morning. Mounting the tandem, they thrust their left feet into the toe clips. Right legs swing over the top tube. They push themselves off on their right feet, seat themselves on their saddles, insert their right feet into the clips, and set off down the macadam. It is a classic tandem start with toe clips. The morning goes nicely. They find they can pedal easier in both their 100 and their 83 gears. This pleases them, and they easily reach the glade for their noon meal. As usual, they execute the classic tandem dismount, pulling their feet out of the toe clips without difficulty. But as they set off again Eve complains to Adam that the nylon clips are rubbing against her toes. At first Adam scoffs, but soon he too begins to feel bruised areas on his feet.

By the time they return to their home base Adam and Eve are unhappy campers.

Not surprisingly, after their evening manna the boa constrictor appears again.

"So kids," he asks cheerfully, "how did it go today?"

"My toes are sore," complains Eve."

"My feet hurt," says the unhappy Adam."

"Now, how in the world did that happen?" asks the disingenuous reptile.

"The toes clips! They rub against our toes!"

"That's too bad," hisses the snake, his tail quivering with repressed delight. "I guess you're just going to have to get bicycling shoes. They'll protect your feet from the toe clips." Adam and Eve are naïve but they are starting to recognize a pattern.

"What are bicycling shoes?" asks Adam.

"Oh, they're like a second skin that fits over your feet. You'll have them between the toes clips and your toes. They'll protect your feet and they'll feel good."

"OK," says Adam, "bring us some bicycling shoes."

"Sorry kids," says the snake breathlessly, "I don't have any. You'll have to get those from God."

CHAPTER FOUR

Baron Karl von Drais may have had a eureka moment while ice skating, recognizing that the momentum supplied by his legs to the skate's gliding runners could be imitated on dry land by a wheeled device; at least, this is the principle he alludes to in the brochure he produced in 1818. Or perhaps he simply conjured up his *laufmaschine* (running machine) out of thin air—he was, after all, an inventor, and the opening decades of the nineteenth century were fertile times for the conception of novel machines of locomotion. Personal transportation still depended on the horse, as it had for millennia, despite a number of inventions designed to replace that long-suffering beast of burden with the power of human arms, legs, or both. Drais himself had come up with one of them earlier, a conveyance seating two to four people, one cranking gears by hand and another steering. This machine was quickly consigned to the dustbin of history.

But a few years later Drais, who lived in Karlsruhe, Germany, developed a clever new contraption. It consisted of two 27-inch diameter iron-shod wooden wheels, placed one behind the other, and connected by a shaped wooden beam (had his invention been considerably smaller, and attachable to the foot, we would have called it an in-line skate.) Large wood forks descended from the beam at either end, to connect to the hubs of the wheels. On top of the beam was a saddle upon which the rider sat, and in front of him was a padded board against which he rested his forearms. Steering, such as it was, was effected by grasping a handlebar attached to a pole, which in turn was connected to the front of the frame. Braking, more or less an afterthought, was accomplished by contacting the ground with the feet. If the machine had had cranks and pedals we would have called it a bicycle; but the rider put it into motion by walking or running. It was, in other words, kick-propelled, and once it was rolling the legs were raised slightly off the ground until a further burst of momentum was needed. For this invention Drais was awarded the equivalent of a German patent. Soon after he claimed a French patent as well, and to the delight of much of the rest of Europe, his invention became international.

Just as a series of pulleys reduce the effort needed to raise a weight, the kick-propelled *laufmaschine* reduced the effort needed to get from one point to another. Drais proved the efficiency of his machine several times in 1817, demonstrating that a rider could not only impel himself at a pace roughly twice that of walking, but could, with considerably more effort, match the speed of a galloping horse. Going down hill the rider could keep both feet in the air and coast, at a substantial saving of effort. But this dangerous maneuver, said Drais, should be attempted only by the most skilled riders. Of course, down hills are almost inevitably followed by up hills, which, with the 50-pound machine under him, would require considerably more effort for the rider to traverse. The *laufmaschine* was sometimes called an "accelerator," since it sped up the act of running or walking; but more popularly, it was known as a "velocipede," (Latin for "fast foot"), since it added velocity to one's natural gait. It was also called the "draisene," a sobriquet derived from the inventor's name.

There was a certain natural attraction to the velocipede: it became the horse. But the rider also became the horse, since he had to furnish the motive power. To a working man that would not be a problem; he was used to being the horse, and could certainly have benefited from the draisene's ability to get around at a faster pace than by foot. But the machines were expensive, outside the reach of the average worker. They became the playthings of those who could not only afford them, but who could also afford to own and use horses. Hence the draisene gained currency with the idle rich, who looked on it as an amusing device that provided some healthy exercise. But it never caught on as a realistic mode of transportation, mostly because it required a dry hard-packed road for its effectiveness. If the path was wet or muddy, the rider became the horse in a literal sense, since he now had to carry his velocipede. As with most amusing but impractical devices, people soon lost interest, and on the continent the draisene craze was essentially over by the end of 1818. For a while, however, it lived on elsewhere.

Denis Johnson, a London carriage maker, began making an "improved" and certainly a more elegant-looking and lighter velocipede, using iron instead of wood for the frame. Johnson also provided a handle attached to the hub of the front wheel, making steering more practical. London society—and indeed, gentlemen and even ladies from all over the island—were enamored with the contrivance, which quickly became known as the "hobby horse" or "charger," and its riders labeled as "dandies." It was so popular that Johnson opened a hobby horse riding school, to which gawkers would flock to observe the gentry learning to operate their machines, with the proprietor usually on hand to take orders. But, as had happened in Paris, the hobby horse was seen as a plaything of the gentry, and it came to be considered a threat to pedestrian traffic. The problem was the same everywhere: the velocipede required a smooth surface in order to operate with any efficiency. Lacking that, riders were wont to take to the sidewalks, where they were uniformly regarded as a menace. Hobby horses did gain a certain currency as racing machines, and contests were organized with some success. Nevertheless, its popularity waned as people tired of the novelty, and by the end of 1919, after the London College of Surgeons warned of serious medical consequences that could result from riding hobby horses, enthusiasm for the velocipede dried up in England. Denis Johnson went back to making carriages.

The New World provided the setting for the final hurrah of Draise's machine. The velocipede arrived in the United States at the end of 1818, built by the Baltimore piano maker James Stewart, who dubbed it the "tracena," a corruption of draisene. For a while it found favor in Philadelphia, New Haven, Baltimore, Boston, and New York, where it was seen as an item of recreation and novelty. As in Europe, it was noted that the machine worked well as long as the ground was level and the path was smooth, but with the primitive condition of American roads this utopian circumstance was rarely encountered. Hence, despite some pockets of interest here and there, by 1821 the craze for the tracena had run its course, and Stewart went back to making pianos. Nevertheless, the velocipede had its impact, and sporadic efforts to improve it would continue to be made.

Draise was probably enough of an engineer to realize that the principle of the gyroscope, in which the angular momentum of a spinning wheel resists efforts to change its course, was the factor that enabled the velocipede to remain upright, as well as to maintain forward motion between foot strokes. It is the same principle that prevents a moving bicycle from falling over, and it is used for the same purpose in ships as well as in airplanes and spacecraft. In fact, it was the wedding of the gyroscopic effect of the spinning wheel to the minimalist approach of the two in-line wheels of his velocipede that was Draise's great contribution to the world of self-propelled transportation. But it would be another 40 years before his concept was realized in a practical way.

CHAPTER FIVE

"And the Lord God commanded the man, saying, "you may eat freely of every tree in the garden; but of the tree of the knowledge of good and evil you shall not eat, for in the day that you eat of it you shall die." (Genesis, 2:16, 17)

Eden is on fire, a hellish inferno. Flames, smoke, soot, and sparking detritus reach to the heavens, swept aloft by powerful updrafts. The sound is deafening as trees, vegetation, animals, birds, and insects are instantly consumed by the crazed flames, sizzling and popping as the water that makes up 90 percent of life is vaporized in great clouds of superheated steam. Birds are destroyed in mid-flight. Animals large and small are shrieking in pain, their last sounds before they are devoured by the firestorm. The popping of exoskeletons, as the denizens of the insect world are boiled in their own juices, adds a machine gun-like undercurrent to the unholy din. The waters are searing roils of haze, poaching their inhabitants alive. The odor of smoldering flesh, commingled with that of burning leaves, bark, cambium, and vegetation of all sorts, is overwhelming. The flames reach temperatures of thousands of degrees as they claw their way into the blood-red sky. The earth itself is burning.

Adam and Eve are in the center of a 10-foot circle of calm, the fire raging uncontrollably around them. As far as they can see, the heavens, the earth, and all they know are ablaze. But Adam and Eve are not seeing very much. They are on their knees, cowering on the ground, foreheads pressed tight to the earth, arms rigidly encircling their heads, as they futilely attempt to ward off the fiery shower of ashes, stones, branches, and sparks that fall in the circle. Their skin is blistered from the intense heat surrounding them, and pockmarked with their smoldering wounds. Their hands are over their ears in a useless effort to protect themselves from the deafening cannonade of the fire. Their eyes are shut desperately tight, but the hot white flames still burn through to their retinas. Their lungs are filled with smoke. Their sphincters have given way in fear and terror and they are kneeling in their own shit. The heat is unbearable.

They are in excruciating pain. They are in utter agony.

Above it all can be heard the voice of God, emanating from the conflagration itself. Its volume fills the universe and it smites Adam and Eve to their very beings with its terrible reverberations. If they knew about death they would be certain they were about to die; in fact, they would be wondering why they were not already dead. Adam and Eve have asked for bicycling shoes and they have offended the Almighty.

"ADAM! EVE! I GIVE YOU A GOOD LIFE. ALL I ASK IS THAT YOU RIDE YOUR TANDEM THROUGH EDEN. THAT IS ALL I REQUIRE OF YOU. I PROVIDE EVERYTHING FOR YOU. I GIVE YOU MANNA TO EAT. I GIVE YOU COOL, CLEAR WATER TO DRINK. YOU HAVE A FINE TANDEM BICYCLE WITH TEN SPEEDS TO RIDE. YOU WANT FOR NOTHING. NOW YOU HAVE THE TEMERITY TO ASK ME FOR BICYCLING SHOES. WHY DO YOU WANT BICYCLING SHOES?"

Adam is shaking so violently he can barely talk.

"The-the s-s-snake s-s-said the sh-sh-shoes would pro-protect our f-f-feet from our t-t-toe clips. The t-t-toe clips hurt our f-f-feet."

"THE SNAKE BROUGHT YOU TOE CLIPS. YOU SHOULD NOT HAVE ACCEPTED THEM! WHY DID YOU ALLOW HIM TO GIVE YOU THOSE TOE CLIPS?"

"The-the s-s-snake s-s-said it would m-m-make it e-easier to p-p-pedal." Adam is beginning to suspect that accepting the toe clips may not have been the best idea.

"TOE CLIPS IS ONLY PART OF IT! THE WORSE THING IS THAT THE SNAKE HAS REVEALED SPEECH TO YOU. I DID NOT INTEND THAT YOU USE YOUR POWERS OF SPEECH. WHY DID YOU ALLOW THE SNAKE TO REVEAL SPEECH TO YOU?"

Eve is terrified. "The s-s-snake came and t-t-talked to us, and we f-f-found that we could t-t-talk, too."

"AND NOW THE SNAKE TOLD YOU TO ASK ME FOR BICYCL-ING SHOES.

"The-the s-s-snake t-told us you'd g-g-give them to us."

"WHY DO YOU PAY ATTENTION TO THE SNAKE? DO NOT LISTEN TO HIM! THAT BOA IS NOT TO BE TRUSTED. BY YOUR SPEECH AND BY YOUR ACTIONS YOU HAVE PUT CREATION IN JEOPORDY. I HAVE HALF A MIND TO START OVER AGAIN."

God is really upset and is threatening to wipe out the universe and start anew; but he thinks twice about destroying his handiwork.

"YOU HAVE NO IDEA HOW DIFFICULT IT IS TO CREATE A UNIVERSE! AND NOW THAT BOA CONSTRICTOR IS RUINING IT ALL! HE REVEALED SPEECH TO YOU; HE GAVE YOU TOE CLIPS; AND HE TOLD YOU TO ASK ME FOR BICYCLING SHOES. I DID NOT PUT FORTH ALL THAT EFFORT JUST TO HAVE IT DE-STROYED BY A SNAKE! I RUE THE DAY I EVER CREATED THAT REPTILE."

God thinks for a long minute as his supplicants suffer in agony. "ALRIGHT. THIS WILL NOT HURT THE UNIVERSE. IT IS A SMALL ITEM AND IT WILL NOT CHANGE ANYTHING. I WILL GIVE YOU BICYCLING SHOES. BUT THAT IS IT, DO YOU UNDERSTAND? I'M TELLING YOU, NO MORE REQUESTS FROM GOD."

God gives in. God should not have done that.

Adam and Eve: "Ye-yes G-G-God, we un-understa-sta-stand."

A millisecond later the fire is gone. Adam and Eve are unharmed. Their skin shows no trace of blisters, or the insidious holes burned in them by falling debris. Their lungs are clear of smoke. Their skin is cool. They feel no pain. The two piles of shit have disappeared. No animal has been harmed. No tree has gone up in smoke. No sea has been turned to vapor. The insects crawl mindlessly on the ground. The birds fill the air and the fish swim in the waters. The grass is its usual green. The temperature is the normal 72 degrees, the humidity the usual 40 percent. The sky is its usual brilliant blue. The air is its usual oxygen-rich mixture. Eden is as it was before. And in the center of the clearing are two pairs of bicycling shoes, black, with red trim, sizes 10-1/2D and 7B.

The shoes are the last word in bicycle touring footwear. The outsoles are made of a synthetic rubber, stiffened to direct the energy of the thrust of the legs into the pedals. At the position of the balls of the feet there are crosswise grooves designed to catch the serrated front edges of the pedals, so that when the straps of the clips are cinched down the feet are properly positioned and locked onto the platforms. The uppers are crafted from a combination of synthetic leather and breathable mesh, skillfully stitched together. The insoles are made of comfortable compressible foam. The toe boxes are designed to protect the extremities from the hard plastic of the toe clips. The inners are intended to cocoon flesh and bone in utmost comfort. Three Velcro straps over the vamps on each shoe secure them to the lower extremities. They have been built on lasts perfectly matching the feet of their intended wearers. Adam and Eve pick them up and examine them. They are items of mystery to the pair, for whom the concept of footwear is totally foreign.

The boa appears in the clearing as the sun begins to sink in the luminous sky. His scaly skin is radiant, and his eyes are glittering. "Hey kids," he breathes sibilantly, "I see you got your shoes."

"You just missed God," says Eve, waving her shoes around. "It was terrible. The sky was on fire. The trees, the grass, the ground, the animals, the insects, the birds, everything was burning. The animals were screaming in pain. The smell was unbearable. Hot embers fell down and burned holes in our skin. We couldn't breathe. The sound was so loud we couldn't think. God was really mad at us and his voice was awful. He was mad at you, too. He said really nasty things about you. He said we shouldn't trust you."

"He scared the shit out of us," adds Adam. "He was mad because we could talk. He was mad at you because you spoke to us and brought us the toe clips and told us to ask him for the bicycling shoes."

"Ahhh," dismisses the reptile, "he's a lot of bluster, like the man behind the curtain, scaring people with smoke and flames. But he's really harmless."

Adam and Eve do not understand the reference to the man behind the curtain, but they let it pass. There is a lot the snake says that they do not understand. There is very little about this situation they understand.

32

Certainly they do not understand God.

"How can you say that?" asserts Eve. "There was nothing harmless about that terrible fire!"

"That so?" asks the snake. "You hurt in any way, Eve? Got holes in your skin from the cinders, Adam? Lungs filled with smoke? Ears hurt? Eyes OK? See any of the animals harmed? Insects look alright? Birds flying OK? Grass OK? Trees still there? And where's your shit?"

Adam and Eve are nonplussed. They have just experienced an unspeakable ordeal that took them beyond the brink of their untested endurance, yet they are completely unharmed. It is as if nothing had ever happened. Not only that, they got their shoes. Who is this God, and why did he find it necessary to frighten them so?

"Who is God anyway?" asks Adam, putting his thoughts into words. "Why does he want to scare us and punish us like that? What did we do to him?"

"Well," hisses the boa, "God is the guy who made all this. He made Eden, he made you, he made Eve, and he made me, too."

"Did he make the lion?" questions Eve.

"Yes, he made the lion and the zebra and all the animals. He made the grass and the trees and the sun and the moon and the stars."

"How did he do that?" she wants to know.

"Easy," the snake replies. "He's omnipotent. He can do anything he wants to do. He can create anything he wants to create. It takes an incredible amount of effort, but once he gets started there's no stopping him."

"If he can do anything he wants than why didn't he want us to have bicycling shoes?" asks the puzzled Eve, somewhat illogically.

"Yeah," says Adam, "and if he didn't want us to talk why did he give us the ability to speak?"

"You have to understand the guy," explains the snake. "He's given you all sorts of abilities. He just doesn't want you to use them."

Adam is becoming annoyed. This is not making any sense. "Why would he give us abilities and not want us to use them?"

"I don't know," hisses the snake, flicking his tongue with excitement, "you'll have to ask him."

Adam and Eve both shake their heads vigorously. "Not on your life," says Adam. "He'll burn us up for sure next time."

The boa shakes his head in return. "Nah, he won't destroy you, no matter what you do. He just wants to scare you. Looks like he did a pretty good job, too."

Adam is thinking this over. The serpent has wounded his burgeoning manly pride. "Well, he didn't scare me that much," he boasts fecklessly. "Maybe he frightened Eve, but I knew all the time it was a trick."

Eve doesn't like Adam's remark. Her assessment is more honest. "Well I was scared," she admits, "I was plenty scared."

Still, Adam has concerns. "God said he was thinking about starting all over. What did he mean by that?"

"He meant that he would make you, Eve, me, all of Eden and everything in it, and the sun and the moon and the stars all disappear. The whole enchilada. Then he would create a brand new universe. He'd start all over."

Despite his earlier attempt at bravado, Adam is frightened at the thought of disappearing into nothingness. "Do you think he'd really do that?"

"Nah," replies the snake, "he's already worked too hard on this one. It cost him too much. Creating this universe was one unbelievably humongous major effort, even for an omnipotent. It took time and it really emptied him out. He's not going to go through all that again unless he absolutely has to."

This reassures the pair, who are gradually being introduced to the concepts of existence and non-existence. At any rate, they are tiring of this metaphysical discussion. Their new shoes are a more immediate topic. They look down at the footwear still in their hands, and Adam holds his pair out for the snake's inspection.

"What do we do with these?" he asks.

"You put them on your feet," is the reply.

Adam and Eve look at each other, mystified. They have no idea how to comply with the snake's instructions.

"Sit down," commands the snake, and they sink to the grass.

"Grab those three tabs and yank," instructs their tutor. "Now slip the shoes onto your feet and pull the tabs back the other way."

Compared to installing toes clips, getting into shoes is easy, now that they understand. In a trice Adam and Eve are shod and walking around on their cushioned bicycling foot ware. They can hardly wait for the next day's ride.

CHAPTER SIX

I ride a classic road bike. The frame, rims, and drop handlebars are aluminum, and the fork is made from carbon fiber. The one-inch wide tires take 120 pounds of pressure. I have a triple chain ring up front and an eight-speed rear cluster, giving me a drive train of 24 gears. The indexed shifting is in the brake levers. It's a mean machine. As the name suggests, it's designed to be ridden on the same surfaces traveled by cars, trucks, and buses. The carbon fork absorbs a lot of the shock of the constant potholes, and even though the thin tires are pumped hard with 120 pounds of air pressure, they're thick enough to grab some road, but not so wide that I lose a lot of energy to friction. The 24 gears give me good selection, although, as is always the case, there's so much overlap that only about 15 are useful. Indexed shifting means that all I have to do to up shift a gear is swing the brake lever sideways. To down shift, I just press a little button next to the brake lever with my thumb. These small movements are enough to derail the chain and put it on the next ring up or down, right into position. It's a great improvement over the old friction shift levers inherited from racing bikes, where you had to guess the correct chain placement, then wiggle the shifter until you got it right. I use a touring saddle with a gel pad—it's not as wide as a cruiser saddle, but not as narrow as a racer's, and the pad does help my butt during those long hours. I use platform pedals, toe clips, and touring shoes. The platforms aren't as efficient as clipless pedals, where your pedals have projections that mate with holes in your shoes, but with all the stop-start riding I do, they're safer. Besides, there have been times when I've had to literally leap off the bike to avoid getting hit, and you can't do that with clipless pedals.

My bike is built for both speed and comfort, and that's the combination I want as a messenger. It's a nimble bike: it gets me out of tight spots and lets me charge ahead when I see a hole in the traffic, yet it's a wheel I can ride all day long. It's fairly light-weight, too, and that makes a difference when you're in the saddle for that length of time. But it's not the best road bike on the market. It would be foolish for me to be messengering with a really light-weight bike and top-notch components; it's almost foolish of me to be riding the one I do, because messengering really beats up your machine. In winter the combination of snow, salt, and sand eats into your drive train like a hungry dog lighting into his kibbles. There are times when only half your gears are working, and you consider yourself lucky to have those. If you don't clean your components every couple of days—every day would be even better—you're going to find yourself sitting on the curb with a busted chain or a broken cable in your hands. The last thing I feel like doing when I get back to my apartment at night is clean off my bike and oil the drive train, but I do it religiously. That bike is my livelihood. Seasons aside, a messenger's bike takes real punishment. Bearings go, gears wear out, cranks fracture, cables snap, chains split, welds give way, spokes break, pedals shatter, stems crack—there's no end to it. Some messengers have spare bikes they can ride when their main machine is in the shop, but that's a luxury I can't afford.

Messengers ride all sorts of bikes. Many have machines like mine, and some have even more expensive—and more delicate—mounts. Some pare their bikes down to a minimum, with only a few gears or no gears at all. It's true that the need for lots of gears isn't that great on the city streets, but I like to be able to drop into a high gear and stomp on the pedals when I have the opportunity, and sometimes I feel like spinning in a 60 gear just for a change of pace. And when you're moving into a stiff head wind it's nice to be able to downshift. But the minimalists don't think that way. To them, anything more than a frame with saddle, wheels, chain, handlebars, and brakes (and some even dispense with brakes) is superfluous. Maybe they're right, because it's usually the people who have been at this longest who ride those one-speeds.

A lot of the guys use mountain bikes. These machines have the virtue of strength. With 26-inch diameter wheels, fat, low-pressure tires, flat handlebars, and a low center of gravity, these rigs are designed for careening down mountain paths. They can't make time on the streets the way a road bike can, but they're practically bullet-proof, and that's a real advantage. The ATB, or "All Terrain Bike," a tame version of the mountain bike, is another popular messenger machine. Like the mountain bike it has the smaller wheels and flat handlebars, but the tires are a little narrower and the bike can make more speed. A few of the messengers ride hybrids, a sort of cross between an ATB and a road bike. They're fine for taking a Sunday afternoon outing, or for cycling on trails, or even for commuting; but I don't favor them for messengering. As the name suggests, the hybrid combines features of both types of bikes, but ends up being neither. Then there's the BMX. That's essentially a kid's one-speed dirt bike, developed for the sport of Bike Moto Cross. The knobby tires are small—only 20 inches in diameter, and it has coaster brakes—you stop by rotating the pedals backward. I've only seen one messenger ride a BMX, although I'm sure there are others. He was an old-timer named Skip Flan, and we all kidded him about his mount. But I'll grant you this: Skip was a strong rider and really made time on his BMX.

It takes a special breed of messenger to ride a cruiser—the old newsboy's bike that my grandfather had as a kid. The classic version is a one-speed machine with coaster brakes and humongous tires, and it weighs a ton. A few updated cruisers will have a Sturmey-Archer three-speed internal rear hub—really old technology, but it's hard to beat the fact that those gears are protected from the elements and they're reliable. They're still big, heavy bikes, though. Why a few of the guys want to ride those heavy steeds I'll never know, but they have everyone's respect.

There are two types of bikes no messenger would ride—recumbents and racers. A recumbent has a lot going for it. It's more comfortable because you're essentially sitting on a canvas seat with a back rest and you're not bending over the handlebars. They're fast, too. But recumbents ride close to the ground, and they're not as nimble as conventional frames. Even when they sport a flagpole and a waving pennant it's almost impossible to see them in traffic. A messenger riding a recumbent in New York would end up road kill inside a few hours. Racers are built for speed, but they achieve that at the expense of sturdiness. You see those racers tearing up and down mountains in contests like the Tour de France, but you also see lines of support vehicles full of spare wheels, gears, and all sorts of components, with spare bikes mounted on top. A true racing bike wouldn't last a day in the city.

Whatever you ride, the pock-marked streets of New York can shake a bike to pieces. Flat tires are common for messengers, and we all carry patch kits and spare tubes in our bags. Broken cables are another hazard, although we normally don't replace them on the streets. If a rear brake cable fails you still have your front brakes and vise-versa, and if the cable to one of your derailleurs breaks you still have the few gears of the other. When your shift is over you take your machine to your bike shop, or you take it home and do the job yourself. Chains don't break very often, but it pays to keep an eye on them. A stretched chain is inefficient, and it's an accident waiting to happen. You can see why some messengers strip their bikes down to essentials. If there are no gears and no hand brakes, there are no cables. Chains that don't have to derail from one set of sprockets to another are going to last a lot longer. Fatter tires are a lot less likely to get caught in street grates or potholes. But you pay a price for that sparseness in speed and maneuverability.

Winter riding is dangerous when there's snow and ice on the ground. You need to be farther out in traffic than usual, because the area near the curb is a filthy mush of slush, sand, and salt. Often there's nothing to do but get up on the sidewalk because that's the only clear place to ride. For some reason the wags think it's funny to ask if you have snow tires or chains for your bike. I wish I did!

You'd think we'd be freezing our asses off, out there on our machines in the dead of winter, but most of the time the opposite is true. You expend a lot of energy and build up a lot of body heat pushing that bike in the cold, and you deal with that by wearing layers—a few shirts, sweaters, and a jacket. Heavy work pants over the biking clothes are a necessity, with a metal clip, a thick rubber band, or even a tied bandanna to keep your right pant leg from getting caught in the chain. Helmet vents keep a flow of cool, fresh air around your head, but you don't want that in the winter—just the reverse; so I use a cloth cover over my helmet. That blocks up the vents and keeps the warm air around my head from blowing out the back. People we deliver to think we want to come in from the cold, and some of them are pretty nice to us, inviting us to sit for a while and warm up. Usually, though, we can't wait to get out of those over-heated office buildings. But those fingers and toes do get cold, no matter how thick your gloves and socks are.

Summer riding has its dangers, too, like road surfaces that turn to thick pools of sticky, black gunk when the sun cooks the asphalt, or the constant need to steer around the hazards of the pervasive construction. Sun screen is a must, and I go through a tube a week, putting it on as my sweat washes it off. But the major risk is the heat. When the sun really beats down it gets hot enough to fry the proverbial egg on a sidewalk, and it can fry your brain just as easily. It's important to take in enough water. I carry 20-ounce water bottles in my two cages, and I drink as much as I can stand. On a hot New York day I'll have drained both bottles by noon. I'll refill them from a water fountain somewhere and drink both of those by the time I quit. Even with all that water, the heat sucks the energy out of you, and by the end of my shift I'm bone tired. But that's the life of a messenger.

CHAPTER SEVEN

"Now the serpent was more subtle than any other wild creature that the Lord God had made. He said to the woman, 'Did God say, "You shall not eat of any tree in the garden"?'" (Genesis 3:1)

Adam and Eve are in high spirits: today they ride in their new bicycling shoes. Over their morning manna they chatter on about the footwear, how the shoes prevent the grass from tickling their feet, how they no longer have to be careful to avoid stepping on rocks, how cozy their toes feel, and how protected they'll be in the clips. It's time to begin the day's circumnavigation. Their newly shod left feet are thrust into the toe clips. Right legs swing over the top tube. They push off, seat themselves, insert their right feet into the clips, and slide the metal edges of the pedals into the grooves in the soles. They have managed a classic tandem start with bicycling shoes and toe clips, and they are off in their 100 gear. With the pedals securely locked to their shoes, the footwear is a welcome addition to their cycling capabilities. They can pull up on one pedal as they push down on the other, and the increased power propels them down the macadam at a faster than usual pace. Their legs are spinning and they are eating up the miles. This is fun! They pass the lion, who mildly notes their uncharacteristic good humor. When the pace becomes tiring Adam shifts down to his 83 gear, and they ride in a more relaxed state for a while, drinking in the sights and sounds of Eden as they move along.

The early hours pass without incident; why shouldn't they? What incident could possibly befall Adam and Eve? This *is* Eden, after all. Nevertheless, by mid morning their cheery mood begins to fade, as they recall their harrowing meeting with the Almighty. Once again the pair discuss their puzzlement. It boils down to this: why would God create them with the ability to communicate with speech, yet not want them to speak? Why would God create them with the ability to learn and better themselves, yet want to keep them in ignorance? They struggle with this and finally agree: God is unknowable and the best thing they can do is accept that.

"But why did God yell at us like that?" presses Eve. "That wasn't nice!"

Adam has no reply, not even "that's God's way." Clearly, Adam and Eve are concerned about their relationship with God. The snake said that he created them, and that was confirmed by God himself; but he was cruel to them, and threatened to destroy them. That is unsettling, even if the snake said that God wouldn't follow through on the warning. The snake is another puzzlement to them.

"If God doesn't like the snake why didn't he torture him, the way he tortured us?" wonders Eve.

Adam thinks. This is not an easy question, and he can only conceive of one answer: "that must be God's way," he says unhappily.

The answer doesn't satisfy Eve, but neither of them can think of a better one. "Why does the snake defy God?" continues Eve. "He seems certain that nothing God does will affect him."

Adam does not answer. He has no answer.

Eve persists. "After all, he said that God made him, just as he made us. Why does he get treated differently from us?"

Again, Adam has no reply other than, "that must be God's way." This is not a fulfilling response. As yet they have not considered even more basic questions: Who *is* God? Where did *he* come from? Who made *him*? Neither recalls that just a few days ago they had no questions to consider at all.

Conversation relieves the tedium of long-distance cycling, and in pondering these existential questions the tandem eats up the miles. Before they realize it the pair reach the sylvan glade where their midday refreshment awaits. Adam applies his hand brakes and the bicycle slows to a halt. He and Eve rotate their right pedals to their bottom positions. Both attempt to plant their left feet on the ground, just as before, but their feet are locked into the toe clips. They have neglected to pull up on their shoes to release the front edges of the pedals from the grooves in the soles. The tandem comes to a complete stop, teeters for a moment, and falls over on its left side, taking the riders with it. It is not a classic dismount.

Had they fallen on the soft grass the result might have been different;

but they are still on the macadamized path. Adam lands hard on the side of his head and Eve scrapes her left knee. Their left hands are stinging, pinned between the macadam and the handlebars. Both have bruised left hips. The insides of both their right legs are smeared with chain grease. There is pain, and this time it is not a matter of smoke and mirrors. This time it is not one of God's illusions. This time they have done it. Not without difficulty, they release their feet from the pedals and crawl out from under the machine. They stand, unsteadily. Bright crimson blood is streaming from the bruise on Adam's head and he is howling with pain. Eve is crying, her knee swelling and oozing blood. Nevertheless, her first thought is for her companion, whose face is dripping with the unfamiliar red fluid.

"Adam," she cries, "something is coming out of your head!" Puzzled, Adam swipes at the wound, transferring splotches of the brilliantly-colored matter to his hand. The sight unnerves them both.

"Now it's on your hand!" she gasps. Frightened at this repugnant turn of events, Eve attempts to wipe the sticky stuff off Adam's face, and her hand also comes away covered with the red substance. Adam sees the blood on her hand and the blood from her knee trickling down her leg, and he, too, is frightened. Nevertheless he attempts to comfort Eve, putting his arm around her shoulder and holding her close. Tears are streaming down both their faces. Blood is something outside their limited experience. Its acrid odor confuses and repels them, reminding them uncomfortably of the smell of animal flesh burning in Eden's recent conflagration. They had not expected to encounter that particular olfactory sensation again, and it adds to their discomfort.

For a long while they simply stand there and look at each other, teary, bewildered, scared, angry, hurting, and frozen by indecision. Finally, when they realize that the bleeding has stopped, and that despite their wounds, which are really no more than superficial, that they are still whole and ambulatory, they break apart. In the future, cyclists who sustain trivial wounds of this nature will brush them off as "road rash," remount their machines, and continue to ride. But Adam and Eve have never experienced bodily trauma. While they are not really convinced that what they went through when God burned Eden was no more than illusion, they do know that *that* pain came to a sudden end. *This* pain is unremitting. *This* pain is the real thing. Their bodies ache. Adam's head is throbbing. Eve's hip hurts, and her knee is swollen. They are in shock. They find their manna, sit, and slowly eat an unhappy midday meal. The food they put in their mouths smells of their blood-tainted hands and it repulses them.

There is no after-meal respite today; they used up that time before they ate, crying and staring at each other's blood. After drinking from the stream they retrieve their bicycle from the macadam, finding it undamaged. They mount with unaccustomed difficulty and set off, at a pace considerably slower than their usual 25 miles per hour. Nevertheless, after awhile, as the stiffness leaves their strained muscles and painful joints, they find that they are able to put on more speed; still, they cannot maintain their normal pace of 80 revolutions per minute in their 100 gear. At first they attribute this to the effects of their wounds, but slowly they become aware that there have been worrying changes in Eden since their noonday break. The macadam path no longer slopes at a two-percent downgrade; it now slopes at one percent. The wind at their backs has slowed from 10 miles per hour to five. There has been an increase in temperature from 72 degrees Fahrenheit to 74. The humidity has risen from 40 percent to 50. Although they do not realize it, daylight in Eden is an hour longer than it used to be. Cycling through Eden is not as easy as it had been. Wordlessly, wondering why Eden has changed, they make their way over the macadam, their mood far from the ebullience they were feeling earlier that morning.

Adam and Eve finally reach their home base. They are hot, sweaty, bloody, hurting, and bone tired. Manna is waiting, and they consume it hungrily. Groaning, they lower themselves to the soft grass and fall into a dead sleep. The next morning finds them still tired and aching. They eat their manna, expecting the serpent to appear. He always does, when things go wrong, and they are not disappointed. No sooner do they finish their last mouthful when he comes gliding out of the underbrush, trying in vain to do a little dance on his pitifully tiny legs.

"Whoa! What happened to you two? You look like hell, both of you!"

"We had an accident," says Adam, glaring at the snake. "We came to a stop at midday, but the grooves in the shoes were caught on the edge of the pedals and we couldn't get our feet out of the toe clips."

"The tandem fell right on top of us," adds Eve. "Adam damaged his head on the macadam and I hit my knee."

"It hurt, and a red liquid came out," complains Adam bitterly.

"Ah," dismisses the boa, "it was just a little blood."

"What is blood?" Eve wants to know.

"Oh, it's just that red liquid matter you were talking about. It goes round and round inside your body. Keeps you warm at night. Stuff like that. Doesn't hurt you to lose a little. Why don't you wash it off? In fact you could both use a bath. Just jump into the stream."

"Why would we want to jump into the stream?" asks Adam suspiciously. Bathing is a concept foreign to the pair, although since the boa constrictor showed up everything has been a foreign concept. Besides, immersing oneself in the liquid one normally partakes of internally seems like a strange thing to do.

"Well, you don't actually have to *jump* in. You can ease yourself in, like this." With those words the snake slithers into the water, swims around a bit, emerges, and rolls around on the grass to dry himself. "See? Nothing to it, and it will clean off all the blood, sweat, and chain grease. Take your shoes off and give it a try."

Eve goes first, sliding cautiously into the clear, waist-high, moving stream. The combination of cold and wet is a new sensation, but not an unpleasant one. Seeing Eve's success, Adam enters the water. At first they merely splash around a bit, but then they realize they can clean the grime, sweat, and blood off their bodies by rubbing the clear fluid against their skin. Adam gets the dried blood off his head and face, and Eve washes her leg. They emerge damp and visibly refreshed and dry themselves on the grass. This latest idea of the snake is not bad! Adam's belligerence toward the boa evaporates.

"That was nice," he says, sitting up.

But Eve asked worriedly, "Do you think God will mind that we did that?"

"Of course not," replies the reptile. "He won't care, and besides, you think all he has to do is watch what you do?"

Adam decides it's time to ask the snake some of the questions he and Eve have been pondering.

"Snake, why did God give us the power of speech if he didn't want us to use it?" Adam forgets that he asked that same question yesterday, so he should not be surprised that he gets the same answer.

"That's his way. That's just the way he is."

The answer is as unsatisfactory today as it was yesterday, but Adam doesn't know how to challenge it. He decides to ask another.

"Why did God treat us so cruelly?"

"Isn't that obvious?" sneers the snake. "I told you yesterday: he wanted to frighten you. He did a good job, too."

Adam pointedly ignores that last remark. "You told us that God made you, just as he made me and Eve, but he treats you differently. He tortured us when we asked for the shoes, but he didn't torture you, even though it was your idea. He was really mad at you for that, and for giving us toe clips and for allowing us to discover that we have speech." This is not exactly a question, but the boa gets the point.

"I have a different relationship with God than you do," he answers.

"What sort of relationship?" asks Eve.

The boa's scaly brown skin takes on a reddish cast. "I don't want to talk about that," he mutters, averting his eyes. "That's between me and the Big Guy."

"Why don't you want to talk about it?" urges Eve unwisely.

The snake's friendly character suddenly vanishes. He rears up on his coiled body, his tail twitching, his flattened head weaving back and forth, his beady eyes boring directly into Eve's, his forked tongue flicking within inches of her nose, his breath hot and fetid. Tiny, dull-red horn-like

46

protrubences appear on the top of his head and he is plainly angry.

"I told you, that's between me and God! It's our business, not yours!" he hisses aggressively at the rattled Eve.

But then, having made his point, the snake settles down. "Now stop asking me these dumb questions. I need to tell you about helmets, unless you want to hurt those tender heads of yours again."

Adam is curious. He waves Eve away from the reptile. "What are helmets?"

The snake has returned to his normal genial self. "A helmet is a hard-shell device you wear on your head when you ride the tandem," he says. "It protects you when you fall. That can happen any time, falling. If you were wearing a helmet yesterday you wouldn't have hurt your head. All bicyclists wear helmets."

That sounds fine, but experience is a good teacher, and Adam is an apt student. He knows what comes next. "And I suppose if we want helmets we'll have to ask God for them!"

"Of course," replies the boa, flicking his forked tongue gleefully. And with that he is gone, before either of them remembers to ask him what he meant by "all bicyclists." But that trivial point is buried under greater concerns.

"No, Adam!" pleads Eve, visibly upset. "Not God. Don't ask God for helmets. God will be angry. God will torture us again. He'll burn Eden to the ground. He'll make us not exist."

Adam also has no desire to go through another of God's infernos, even though he's inclined to believe the snake on the point of the viability of their existence. Still, he reasons, a helmet sounds like it could be a valuable asset. It might be worth the temporary pain that God would dish out. Besides, how bad was it—and anyway, it was all an illusion. The snake said so. He tries to convince his companion.

"Eve, we *need* those helmets! You heard the snake—we could fall on our heads at any time. You have no idea how much that hurt, and I wouldn't want that to happen to you." Adam's concern for Eve is touching, but she is still not convinced.

"Come on, Eve, how bad will it be? We weren't really hurt last time, and I don't think he'll wipe out the universe."

But this is not the time to call God; this is the time to get on the road. Left feet are thrust into toe clips. Right legs swing over the top tube. They push themselves off, seat themselves, and insert their right feet into the clips. They lock the front edge of their pedals into the grooves in the soles of their shoes. It is a classic tandem start with toe clips and bicycling shoes. Despite their injuries from the previous day, despite their tiredness, despite the changes in the incline of the path, the decrease in the speed of the wind, and the increase in temperature, humidity, and the length of the day, the shoes and toe clips do help, and they manage to complete their assigned circumnavigation before dusk. They remember to lift their shoes out of the pedals before they dismount and they get through the day without incident. They have a bath in the stream before bedtime and enjoy a good night's sleep.

The next morning, over manna, Adam offers a compromise. "I'll tell you what: we'll ask God for helmets. If he says he's going to wipe us out and start all over again we'll just tell him that we really don't want the helmets after all. He won't take away our existence if we really don't want them."

Eve is still doubtful, but Adam sounds so assured that she gives in. Adam wastes no time.

"God!" he shouts to the heavens. "This is Adam. We'd like to talk to you, me and Eve."

For a long moment there is no response. Suddenly a walnut tree not five feet from the couple bursts into flames. Eve clutches Adam's arm and begins to sob. It's going to happen all over again—Eden will be destroyed. But Eve is wrong. Only the one tree burns, although it is a roaring conflagration, sending forth a vicious heat that drops the supplicants to their knees in fear. From within the tree comes God's booming voice. It fills their bodies with trepidation; but it does not fill the universe, the way it did last time.

"Adam, Eve, I Have Given You Everything You Need. What Do You

Want Now?"

"God, I hope you've been well," snivels Adam, hoping to curry a little favor.

"Do Not Waste My Time!" thunders God. "What Do You Want?"

"Well, God," begins a chastised Adam, "our tandem fell down and I hit my head. Blood came out. It hurt. The snake said we need helmets to protect our heads. The snake said that we could fall down again and. . ."

"The Snake! The Snake! Always The Snake! Let Me Ask You Something, Eve. Why Did Adam Hit His Head?"

Eve knows the answer to that one. "Because the tandem fell down."

"And Why Did The Tandem Fall Down?" God is leading Eve down a Socratic path.

"Because we didn't get our shoes out of the pedals in time."

"And Why Did You Need To Be Wearing Shoes?"

"Because the toe clips hurt our toes."

"And Why Did You Need Toe Clips?"

Eve is silent—she can't remember. Why *did* they need toe clips? Things were just fine without them, weren't they? The flames shoot up a little higher. It is only one tree but Adam and Eve are getting toasted.

"Humph!" says God. "I Rest My Case. What I Really Should Do Is Take Back Your Toe Clips, Your Shoes, And Your Speech! I Should Send You Back To Zero. Ah, But That Would Be Too Much Work! Well, We Are Too Far Along Here To Turn Back. Alright, You Can Have Your Helmets. But No More Demands From God, Do You Understand?"

With a final burst of searing flame the fire extinguishes itself and life in Eden is back to normal. The tree is unharmed, its leaves as green as ever, beetles crawling on its bark, birds singing in its branches. It is, in other words, a normal Garden of Eden walnut tree, except that out of its branches tumble two white bicycle helmets. Adam picks them up, elated.

"That was easy," he crows. "He gave in right away. We got a little hot from those flames, but he didn't really torture us, not like last time. He didn't threaten us. Although he did seem to be mad at the snake again."

Eve is much relieved, and her opinion of Adam's judgment goes sky high. "You were *right*, Adam," she says admiringly. "That *was* easy. Except—why *did* we need the toe clips in the first place?"

But Adam is not listening. He is too busy examining the head gear. They are made from materials the pair have never seen: plastic outer shells with foam liners. Inside they see indecipherable characters: "Meets the CPSC bicycle helmet standard". The helmets have several large vents, designed to allow a free flow of air to the wearers' heads. Straps with plastic buckles dangle from their sides. Adam hands the smaller one to Eve and they place the protective devices on their heads. They have been carefully sized and fit precisely, but they have no idea how to fasten the dangling straps.

Adam says, "don't worry. The snake will show us how."

Right on cue, the boa crawls out of the jungle. He is working hard to hide the smirk on his face.

"So, God gave you the helmets, huh?"

"Yes," says Adam jubilantly. "He didn't give us any trouble at all. He didn't even set Eden on fire—just one tree. He did seem to be mad at you, though."

"Yeah, he's always gonna be a little mad at me," muses the snake. "Looks like you need a little help getting those straps fastened." The snake issues instructions and the pair quickly learn how to buckle their helmet straps.

You kids look great in those helmets. Well, I'll see you later," he calls as he disappears into the underbrush, no longer bothering to hide the smirk.

Days and weeks pass. Eden has changed. Now there is no incline in the path at all: Adam and Eve are pedaling on a flat road. The tail wind has disappeared altogether. The temperature is a few degrees warmer, and the humidity has increased again. They do not understand how these changes have taken place, and at any rate, there is little they can do about them. They perspire regularly now, and drink more water when they stop. But their bodies have grown stronger, meeting the demands of the new conditions. Wearing their shoes and their helmets, they still cycle 200 miles every day; but they can no longer maintain a pace of 25 miles per hour. They can no longer circumnavigate Eden in eight hours of riding. It now takes ten; still, they do not notice because the days have become correspondingly longer. They still rest one day out of seven. They bathe in the stream daily. Their wounds have healed. They no longer concern themselves about God. The boa constrictor no longer visits them. Eden has changed and Adam and Eve have survived.

CHAPTER EIGHT

The notion of adding cranks and pedals to the front wheel of a drai-sene, as elemental as it might seem now, eluded inventors for some 40 years. The breakthrough occurred in Paris, although exactly when, and by whom, is not entirely clear. Pierre Lallement, a mechanic working for a carriage maker, claimed that he built the first true bicycle in 1863, when he was 20 years old, and learned to ride it by practicing in a long hallway in his employer's shop. Two years later Lallement sailed for America, bringing the parts for one of his new machines with him. He assembled his contraption in Connecticut, where he introduced it to the bewildered local population. A year later he obtained the only patent ever filed on the basic bicycle, an event that will assume some importance in the history of that machine. Two years after that, having failed to find a backer for his mechanical horse, the disappointed Lallement returned to France. But that's not the end of his story; we'll hear from the inventor again.

An alternate version of the origin of the pedaled two-wheeler holds that it was the brainchild of the Parisian blacksmith Pierre Michaux; that he first conceived of the idea in 1861; and that he produced his first bikes in 1867. Other evidence suggests that Michaux's bicycle was developed not by him but by two young engineering students working with Michaux's younger brother Ernest, and that Ernest and Lallement also worked together. This confusion has never been sorted out, but no matter; Lallement's and Michaux's contraptions were much alike, suggesting that at least one of the parties was familiar with the other's work. Whatever the truth, by 1868 Michaux had a factory with 60 workmen producing bicycles, and was filling orders all over Europe.

Similar to a draisene in general aspect, the machine had cranks and pedals attached to the front wheel's hub. The wheels were bigger than those on its kick-propelled predecessor, between 30 and 35 inches, with the front larger than the rear, since the greater the diameter of the wheel the more ground that could be covered by one revolution of the pedals. The rider sat on an adjustable saddle attached to a wrought-iron serpentine frame that replaced the draisene's wooden beam. At first the wooden wheels were shod with iron rims, but by the end of the decade solid rubber tires were added, somewhat moderating the harsh ride. Hubs with ball bearings also appeared at this time, allowing pedaling with less effort. Braking was achieved by restraining the motion of the pedals with the feet, or with a primitive hand brake. Despite the profoundly different method of propulsion—pedaling instead of kicking—the new machine took the name of the old: "the velocipede."

With the simple addition of cranks and pedals it was possible for a rider to propel himself forward continually, balancing himself and his machine with the aid of the gyroscopic effect of the rotating wheels. Nevertheless—and to say the least—the machine had some drawbacks, the major one being the method of mounting. The rider jogged with the velocipede to get it rolling; then, when a minimum velocity had been reached, he would vault onto the saddle, his feet searching for the pedals mounted on the orbiting cranks. Another imperfection was that unlike modern bicycles, the pedals did not freewheel, but continued to revolve as long as the wheel rotated. Hence, each leg was drawn up and then extended, making it all too possible in a turning maneuver for the rider's body to come into contact with the front wheel, or for the foot to slide into the spokes. And finally, as heavy as the old draisenes were, the pedaled versions weighed nearly twice as much—about 70 pounds. Still, once the rider got all that mass moving, the effort required to balance one's self and propel the bike forward on a good, level road was not beyond the abilities of the average healthy person. Under these ideal conditions speeds up to 10-12 miles per hour were possible.

Velocipedes were expensive, and like the earlier draisenes, became playthings of the rich. They were purchased and used by those who also had carriages and horses, but who enjoyed riding around the boulevards, getting a little healthy exercise while showing off their expensive toys. And as with the draisene, the workmen who would have benefited most from owning velocipedes could scarcely afford them. Nevertheless, the velocipede developed a far greater following than its predecessor, and one of the reasons was the macadamization of many of Paris's major streets. More than anything else, it was the presence of these smooth, rutless surfaces that spurred the sales of Michaux's machines.

The velocipede craze in France reached its peak in 1869, with thousands of the mechanical horses in service and scores of makers scattered around the country. Among these was Pierre Lallement himself, who had sold his American patent and used the money to open a shop. Nevertheless, the velocipede was destined to follow a course similar to the one that befell the draisene. As the machines became a more frequent sight their status changed from novelty to nuisance. Accidents were frequent. Cyclists regularly collided with pedestrians and frightened horses, and the public resented the sight of young gentry tearing around town with little regard for their own or anyone else's safety. France's love affair with the two-wheeled machine came to an abrupt end in 1870, with the Franco-Prussian war, when bicycle manufacturers were forced to turn to armament making. Still, there had been many advances in bicycle design during those heady years, including the advent of solid rubber tires, wire spoking, improved bearings, and lighter frames and wheels.

The first bicycles in England, where they were called "boneshakers," were imported in 1868, from Michaux's factory in Paris. The results were predictable: they were owned and ridden by young men with money, races were organized, exhibitions took place, crowds cheered them on, and the vehicles were promoted as a healthy form of exercise. Although England's excellent network of macadamized roads made racing and long-distance riding feasible, by the end of 1869 cycling no longer had the cachet of adventure and promise. It was clear that a lightweight, inexpensive, and safe velocipede could serve a real need; but the bicycle was not yet able to respond to those requirements.

Cycling in the New World began in 1866, when Lallement assembled his first unit in Connecticut; but it wasn't until two years later, when a troupe of bicycling acrobats toured the country, that it became a fad. As in Europe, the machine was expensive, priced out of the reach of working men. Furthermore, the cost was kept artificially high by a carriage maker named Calvin Witty, who controlled both Lallement's original patent as well as one filed by the cycling acrobats. Thus, Witty held a monopoly on bicycle making in the United States. He demanded a fee for every velocipede sold in the country, assuring that the American product would cost twice the amount of a French machine. Still, for a while, the velocipede prospered in America as an item of amusement. As in Europe, racing drew large crowds; but cycling on the streets and roads of American cities was another story. The growing number of riders came to be considered a menace to normal navigation, scaring horses and knocking down pedestrians. And as with the draisene, the medical world began to predict dire consequences for velocipede riders, including the dreaded fear of losing one's manhood. By 1871 the craze was over.

Aside from the inflated prices, probably the major reason for the failure of the bicycle to catch hold as a genuine item of transportation in the United States was the notoriously poor conditions of most of the nation's unmacadamized roads. Still, in the short time the velocipede obsession held sway, Yankee ingenuity had considerably improved the mechanism, with important innovations such as the tubular frame and the lightweight wire-spoked wheel with rubber tires.

CHAPTER NINE

Adam is perched on the unfamiliar saddle of a bright orange and yellow Trek 1000 solo road bike. He is wearing his helmet and his bicycling shoes are thrust into toe clips attached to platform pedals. A transparent vessel containing an unidentifiable liquid is housed in a metal cage attached to his down tube, but Adam pays it no attention. He is focused on the nimble manner in which his machine handles; this is not his usual tandem, and Eve is not mounted behind him. He recognizes immediately that he is riding on a strange path: this is a smoother surface than the familiar macadam. It is considerably wider and it has an intermittent, broad, yellow line down the middle with equally large white lines on the edges. He sees no jungle at the sides of the road—only grassy ditches followed by open land. He passes fields full of yellow plants on long green stalks. Other areas are populated with low-lying leafy green vegetation. Every so often the fields are interrupted by enormous, outlandish, irregular, box-like structures with paths leading to them, usually colored white, and surrounded by leafy trees. Spotted here and there are odd varieties of four-legged creatures, only vaguely similar to those he has grown accustomed to in Eden. Tall, slender tree trunks, denuded of leaves and branches, line both sides of the road at regular intervals. There are cross pieces near their tops, and they are connected to one another with what appears to be rows upon rows of continuous smooth, black vines. The air smells strange. It is not the oxygen-rich mixture he's used to, and it is faintly fouled with an odiferous ammonia. The sun tells him it is still morning, but it is warmer and more humid than the climate he is used to, and his body is wearing a light coat of perspiration.

In the instant it takes him to make these observations Adam realizes that he is faced with a far greater mystery: he is surrounded by other bicyclists. Hundreds and hundreds of bicyclists. They are all over the path, and only the skills developed by keeping his machine hewed to the center of the macadam (*keep your eyes on the road!*) prevent him from careening into his nearby neighbors. Adam assumes that these creatures are members of his species, since they vaguely resemble him and Eve in their body types, the arrangement of their limbs, and their general appearance. They certainly do not look like any of the monkeys, apes, or other primates he and Eve see in the Garden, and furthermore, they are all wearing bicycle helmets. He is thunderstruck at the very idea that there could be other members of his species. Still, Adam can't be sure. Most of them have large, dark, round or oblong objects covering their eyes, and they all appear to have multicolored skin violently different from his. He sees deep reds, the darkest blacks, blinding whites, glaring greens, intense oranges and bright pinks—the colors are infinite in variety, with indecipherable markings on them, and they all change hue at the biceps, calves, and ankles. He glances down. No, as far as he can see his skin color has not changed and there are no untoward markings on him. All he knows is, this is not the familiar macadam path. This is not his tandem. Eve is gone. He does not know how he got here, he does not know where he is going, and he does not know who—or even what—the other bicyclists are.

Where is he? What strange part of Eden is this? Where is Eve? What is he doing on this bizarre one-person machine, only half a tandem? Why are his lungs straining so? Who are all these creatures surrounding him, some riding alongside, some passing him by, others only plodding along, some on tandems, most on solo bikes like his? Some are obviously of his gender, some clearly of Eve's, and many could belong to either. Where did they come from and why has he never seen them before? Adam is thoroughly bewildered, frightened nearly out of his wits. He would like to stop and try to figure all this out, but rejects that idea. What would he do if he stopped? Where would he go? What would happen to him? Besides, if he stopped he would certainly be hit by one of the riders following close behind him. He has no choice but to keep pedaling and to stay out of the way of these frightening creatures as best he can.

Some of the riders are shouting, and others pick up the cry: "CAR BACK, CAR BACK!" Adam has no idea what the clamor is all about, but the group he is riding near ease their bicycles over to the right, so he does the same. With an ominous rumble, an enormous wheeled vehicle passes him closely on his left. It is as big as an elephant, but smooth and shiny, and the way it reflects the sun hurts Adam's eyes. It seems to be making the same sort of sounds the lion makes with his throat, but it smells of a noxious emission which, combined with oil, gasoline, metal, and paint, is an odiferous combination foreign to Adam. He sees a species member inside—perhaps a male? Yes, a male; but he is not pedaling, and there is no visible means of locomotion. Still, the huge machine easily passes him and the other riders, every once in a while emitting a raucous grunt. It frightens him. Perhaps it *was* an elephant, or some strange other beast. It certainly didn't look like a bicycle, but then again, it had wheels and a man *was* riding it, so what else could it be? Adam knows of no other mode of transportation.

At any rate, his mind is now occupied by a new problem: he is approaching a hill. Adam has never seen a hill before, much less tried to ride up one. All his bicycling experience has been on downgrades and flat roads. His legs would like to be spinning at their accustomed pace of 80 revolutions per minute, but with the torque now required by the grade, and the reduced oxygen content of this strange air, Adam has to work extremely hard just to keep his bicycle moving. He remembers the lesson on gears he got from the snake: a lower gear makes pedaling easier. In fact, the bicycle Adam is riding on has a triple chain ring and an eight-speed rear cluster. He has his choice of 24 gears. But Adam has no idea how to change speeds on this machine, since there are no shift levers visible on the down tube. Adam's legs are burning, his face is flushed, and he is gasping for breath from the effort of riding up what is really a rather mild hill; nevertheless, in his troubled state of mind he scarcely notices his physical distress. "What part of Eden is this? How did I get here?" he keeps asking himself, over and over again. But there is no answer. Adam is trapped in this malefic ride. Then it comes to him, in a flash of insight: God is punishing him again—that must be it! But no—logical fellow that he is, he rejects that explanation. He and Eve haven't asked God for anything since they got the helmets, so why would God be upset with him?

Adam reaches the pinnacle of the hill and is about to get a lesson in gravity. His speed picks up as he starts down the other side. He should stop pedaling and let the bicycle freewheel, but he has never coasted before except when coming to a complete stop, and he doesn't realize he can do it now. He soon reaches a speed of 25 miles per hour, the speed at which he used to circumnavigate Eden, and it is not uncomfortable; but gravity demands that objects with mass accelerate on down hills. As his bicycle goes faster Adam finds himself holding on to the drops of his handlebars for dear life. He is petrified, deathly afraid that he might crash. He still has a vivid memory of the bruises he sustained from his previous accident, and he is aware enough to realize that if his bike falls down at this speed he could suffer some real damage, helmet or no. But he knows where the brake levers are, and he knows how to use them. Still turning the pedals, he squeezes the levers and manages to slow his machine down a little. When the slope levels off he releases the brakes and continues along, although the effort of climbing the hill and the fright of the descent have left him sweating profusely and breathing rapidly.

"CARBACK, CARBACK," comes the call again. Adam slides over to the right and watches another of those immense, shiny, smelly, elephantine machines go past. This one has two people in it, almost certainly a male and a female, so it must be a tandem, even though they are seated side by side. Adam is trying to get a grip on himself. Again, he thinks there must be some connection between what he is experiencing now and what he went through when God burned Eden. But that terrifying experience lasted only for a few minutes, or so it seemed; this has been going on for much longer than that, and shows no sign of coming to an end. Besides, this time no one is talking to him.

"HEY BUDDY, HOW'RE YOU DOIN'?" The words come from a creature riding on his left. Nearly startled out of his saddle, Adam glances over and sees a tall, slender, sinewy young man, a fellow rider, with brown and cream skin, wearing a tan helmet. He is riding a gold-colored machine, similar to Adam's, with practiced ease. Like the others, he has large, dark, oblong objects covering his eyes. Adam wonders how the riders can see the road when their eyes are covered, but they all seem to be doing fine. This rider doesn't appear to be God, but Adam takes no chances.

"Who are *you?*" he asks.

"Name's Jack. What's yours?"

"Adam" he answers, keeping his eyes in front of him (*keep your eyes on the road!*). Adam calls on his powers of deduction: it has speech and it's not a snake, so it *must* be a member of his species, despite its multi-colored skin. He thinks he may be able to get some answers to his questions from his new companion.

"Enjoyin' the ride, Adam?"

But Adam answers with "What part of Eden are we in?"

Jack appears to be nonplussed. "Eden? Well we started in Sergeant Bluff and we're headed for Ida Grove. I don't think we go through Eden."

"But we're *in* Eden!" Adam can't wrap his mind around the possibility that anything exists outside of Eden.

"No, I told you, we're not in Eden. I don't know where that is."

"Then where am I?"

Jack is amused. "What, do you have amnesia or something, Adam? You're in Iowa, on County Road D38. This is the first day of RAGBRAI."

In *Eye-oh-wa?* County Road *dee thirty ate?* The first day of *Ragbray?*

"*Ragbray?* What is *Ragbray?*"

"Did you get on this ride by mistake or something? No—you're wearing a wrist tag, so you must have signed up."

Adam looks down and sees that he is indeed wearing a gray band around his wrist, like everyone else he sees. Still, Jack's answers are of no help at all. Adam presses on.

"What is that terrible smell in the air?"

"Hey, you're *not* from Iowa, are you! That's pig shit. The farmers use it for fertilizer."

Adam knows what "shit" is, although "fertilizer" is not in his vocabulary.

"Are you a farmer?" as if Adam knew what that is.

60

"No, I'm a plumbing contractor."

"Plumbing contractor" is as mysterious to Adam as "farmer," but he has more important questions.

"Who are all these other species members? Where did they come from?"

Jack gets a kick out of that. "Species members! That's a good one, Adam! They're on the ride, same as me and you."

"How can you see anything with those dark things in front of your eyes? Everyone else has them, too."

"Jeez, Adam, they're sunglasses. They protect your eyes from the sun. Haven't you ever seen them? Haven't you ever worn them? Hey, are you OK?"

Adam is not OK, but he takes this as an invitation to tell Jack something of his history.

"I'm from some other part of Eden. That's where Eve and I ride our tandem. The snake gave us toe clips and God gave us bicycling shoes and helmets. Why am I here? Are. . .are you sure. . .you aren't God?"

Jack is amused by this recitation. "Ah, I get it," he chuckles. "Adam—Eve—Eden—Snake—God. Garden of Eden, right? Bible, right? Genesis, right? That's great! Must be some place, where you live. No, I'm pretty sure I'm not God, although I have been called a snake now and then. Ha, ha!"

Adam does not share his mirth. "I need to get back to the other part of Eden, where Eve is."

"Look, I can't help you. I told you, we don't go through Eden, at least not today. I never heard of that town—maybe it's in the Eastern part of the state. Uh, just how *did* you get here?"

"I don't know," replies a miserable Adam, "I'm just here."

As Jack ponders this statement the riders start up another hill, and he sees how Adam is straining to climb.

"Hey Adam," he calls. "Why don't you downshift?"

Downshift! Adam knows about shifting! At last Jack is making sense.

"I can't find the shift levers on this bicycle," he complains.

"They're in the brake levers. Just push your right lever over to the left." Jack demonstrates with his lever.

Adam, of course, doesn't know the meaning of right and left, but following Jack's lead he applies the movement to his brake lever and miraculously, with a soft click, the bicycle downshifts. He moves it again and it downshifts another gear. Despite his confusion Adam is delighted. He is conquering one small corner of this strange environment! Still, he is confused by the clicking noise of the shifting, since the gear levers on the tandem he rides with Eve move silently.

"Why are the gears clicking?" he asks Jack.

"Indexed shifting always clicks."

"What's indexed shifting?"

"That's shifting with individual stops for each gear, so you don't have to adjust your shift lever every time you change. Don't you have that on your tandem back home?"

"I don't think so," replies Adam.

"Well your bike must be an old-timer if it still has friction shifting! Indexed shifting has been around for 20 years now."

Adam has no reply. He doesn't like the idea that his tandem back home is not up to date, but right now there is this hill to climb. Every time Adam hears Jack change a gear, he changes his. The going is slower, his lungs are still heaving, but there is less strain on his legs. "What a wonderful thing this indexed shifting is," he thinks to himself.

They reach the summit and start the descent. Jack stops pedaling, allowing his bicycle to freewheel. Adam has never freewheeled on a down hill before; still, *not* pedaling is a simple skill to master. Both cyclists resume locomotion when they reach the bottom of the hill, and Jack shows him that he can upshift by clicking a little button mounted on the brake lever. Adam does so, and is rewarded with a quick *ker-thunk*. He still does not know where he is or what he is doing here, but he has mastered his gears. He can downshift and he can upshift. He can make those gears go *click* and *ker-thunk*. This pleases him.

Another hill approaches, a steep one. Adam quickly goes through his gears, but it is still tough going.

"Use your granny gear, Adam," calls Jack.

Adam's reply is predictable. "What is my 'granny gear'?"

"That's the lowest gear on your small chain wheel." Jack demonstrates by clicking the button on his left brake lever. Adam follows suit and finds that he is pedaling quickly and moving slowly, but expending a lot less effort.

"This is the gear your grandmother would use if she was riding a bike up this hill," Jack reveals with a chuckle.

"Grandmother?"

"Yeah, your grandmother. Your grandmother? Well, maybe she's dead?"

Adam, of course, has no concept of death. He has no concept of grandmother, either.

Jack sees his bewilderment. "Like, your mother's mother, or your father's mother? You do have a mother, don't you?"

A confused silence is Adam's only reply.

"Come on Adam, you gotta have a mother. Do you have a father?"

Adam seeks enlightenment. "I don't think I have a mother or a father. What are they?"

"They're the people who made you. They brought you into this world."

"You mean God? The snake said God made me and Eve and everything in Eden."

"Well yeah, sure, but I'm talking about your earthly mother and father. Your father fertilized your mother's egg. Your mother gave birth to you."

Adam is confused. Are there yet more people in Eden, fathers, mothers?

"How did they do that?" he queries.

"Well, they had, ah, you know, they made love, just like you and Eve." Jack halts that thought. "Er, is Eve your wife? Your girlfriend?"

"Wife? Girlfriend?"

"Well, do you and Eve ah, make love?" Jack strongly suspects that this conversation is going nowhere.

"Make love?"

Jack thinks he'd better end this lesson on the birds and the bees. "Oh, man! Ah, well, I guess you'll find out eventually."

Jack is as confusing as the snake and God, thinks Adam. He decides to change the subject.

"I'm thirsty," he announces to no one in particular. "I need water"

"Take a drink from your water bottle," offers Jack.

Adam doesn't know what a water bottle is; any sort of container or vessel is outside his experience in Eden.

"I don't see a stream," he replies.

"No, your *water bottle!* Look."

Jack reaches down and draws his plastic water bottle from the cage mounted on his down tube. It is the same arrangement that Adam has; the same arrangement that nearly all the cyclists have. Jack puts the nipple of the plastic bottle between his lips and drinks. Adam hesitates. To follow Jack's example he will have to steer the bike with one hand while the other finds the bottle and guides it to his lips. This is not a good idea— Adam has never steered with one hand. But he glances around and sees that some of his fellow riders are doing just that, with no untoward consequences. He decides to chance it, and is successful in capturing the vessel with his right hand. He raises it to his lips, but no liquid flows into his mouth. Frustrated, he complains to Jack.

"There is no water in this thing!"

Jack sees that he's dealing with a complete tenderfoot. "Grab the nipple between your teeth and pull it open. Then squeeze the bottle."

Adam complies and his mouth is greeted by a welcome stream of liquid. This is fun! He is coolly steering with one hand and drinking water with the other. Adam is multitasking, a new experience. If only Eve could see him now. He drains half the bottle, replaces it in its cage, and returns to two-handed steering, not without a sense of relief. He looks around with a little less than his usual caution and makes another discovery: the

64

colored skin on Jack and the others isn't really skin after all; it is some sort of thin covering. Some of the women, he notes, are partially naked, wearing chest protectors on the upper parts of their torsos. Everyone is wearing some sort of covering for their genitals, but everyone's arms and legs are exposed. One thing is clear to Adam: no one is naked as he. This all puzzles him. Why should Jack and the others want to cover themselves, and what *is* the stuff that covers them? He asks Jack:

"Why aren't you naked? Why is that covering on you?" Once again, Jack seems to be amused.

"Well, these are my clothes. They keep the sun off me, so I don't have to cover my whole body with suntan lotion. And these shorts have a nice bit of padding in the bottom. Helps keep my butt comfortable. Besides, people don't go around naked like you. It's not considered nice and anyway, it's against the law."

Adam is pleased with himself. One more bit of this mystery has been solved. These are *clothes!* That he is breaking the law has no meaning for him. He ventures another question.

"Do you think I should ask God for clothes?"

Jack is laughing out loud now. This fellow Adam is *funny!* But Adam is distracted before Jack can answer.

"IOWA CHOPS! GET YOUR IOWA CHOP HERE!"

The cry comes from a man standing at the rear of one of those enormous gleaming four-wheeled bicycles stopped by the side of the road. It is even larger and more grotesquely shaped than the others he has seen. The man is burning large pieces of flesh on some sort of fire device. The odor sickens Adam: it is what Eden smelled like when God made it an inferno.

"Why is that species member burning flesh?" he calls to Jack. "God does that when he's mad."

"You mean that guy doing pork chops on the grill by the pickup? He's selling them to the bikers. You a vegetarian, Adam?"

But Adam doesn't answer. He is fascinated by the sudden change in the appearance of the terrain. They are approaching a town—Anthon, to be exact—and there are signs of habitation. He sees more strange objects of various sizes—houses, mobile homes, garages, barns, out buildings, lawns, driveways, cars, trucks, tractors, combines, and mowers—in growing profusion, and cannot fathom their purpose. The road is lined with people seated on various strange objects, cheering the cyclists on. There are more vendors on the sides, selling watermelon, lemonade, soft drinks, ice cream, kolaches, corn dogs, hot dogs, and sandwiches, all surrounded by bicyclists consuming their wares. The odors make him hungry; besides, the sun is overhead, reminding Adam that it's lunch time.

"Where is my manna?" he asks Jack. His companion looks at him.

"I don't know. Did you lose it?"

"Eve and I eat it three times every day. It's time for my noon-time manna. How do I find my manna?"

"What does it look like?" asks Jack.

"It's a round cake," replies Adam.

"Ah," says Jack. "I think we'll find some manna here. Just follow me."

They have come into town and are passing the fire station, where a large cardboard sign is leaning against the building:

WELCOME RAGBRAI XXXIV!
ANTHON VOLUNTEER FIRE FIGHTERS PANCAKE LUNCH $5

Five large portable griddles have been set up in front of the station, each capable of cooking 20 pancakes at a time. Each griddle is manned by a fireman, busily pulling completed cakes off the griddles and replacing them with fresh batter. On the right of the line of griddles, a large table is covered with plates of butter, bottles of maple syrup, packets of sugar and whitener, plastic flatware, napkins, paper cups, and large containers of water, lemonade, and coffee. On the left is a table where a seated volunteer with a cash box is taking money. Hundreds of cyclists are milling around, some occupying the few available picnic tables, but most leaning against the fire house or sitting cross-legged on the ground, all eating pancakes off paper plates with plastic forks. Adam does not understand concepts like town, fire station, griddle, or cook, no less paper plates and forks. He has no idea what is going on. But he does recognize that his fellow species members are eating.

Jack pulls over to the fire house and Adam follows him in. He finds it easier to dismount from a solo bike than from a tandem, and remembers to lift his shoes to free them from the pedals before withdrawing them from the toe clips; but that's not where Adam's attention is focused. He is intoxicated by the odor of the pancakes, the mixture of wheat flour, baking powder, sugar, eggs, butter, and milk. The round shape is familiar, but the cakes smell better than manna; they smell better than anything he has ever smelled before. He thinks, "this must be the kind of manna they eat in this strange *Ragbray*." He drops his bicycle to the ground. There is a ragged line of 20 or so riders waiting to buy their lunch, but Adam bypasses them, strides up to the nearest griddle and before anyone can stop him, attempts to remove a pancake. The half-cooked cake falls apart, refusing to be dislodged from the griddle, and he singes his fingers on the hot cooking surface. It hurts! Adam howls. He has still not yet learned to deal with pain. Pain is God's punishment. Bewildered firemen and other cyclists watch as Jack pulls Adam away.

"Jeez Adam, that was dumb. Didn't you know that griddle was gonna be hot?"

Jack pulls the plastic bottle out of the cage on Adam's bicycle and squirts some water on Adam's fingers. Adam knows from experience that a water bath has curative powers, and the pain soon subsides to a dull throb. Jack takes Adam to the end of the line.

"Well I guess you like pancakes, so let's get some lunch," he says. Adam follows Jack to the cashier, and watches as Jack hands over a five-dollar bill. Adam starts to move on but the man behind the table addresses him:

"Ah, that'll be five dollars for the pancakes, sir." The volunteer sees the uncomprehending look on Adam's face and looks at his nude body.

"Sir, are you making some kind of documentary?" He looks around. "Is there a camera crew around here? Is this like that old TV show, 'Candid Camera'?" He makes a command decision and nods his head.

"Well you go ahead and get yourself some pancakes, sir. We wouldn't want anyone out there in TV land to think that Anthon isn't a real friendly little Iowa town."

Adam moves down the line and is handed a paper plate with three large golden-brown pancakes on it. Jack has helped himself to butter, syrup, plastic fork, and napkin, but Adam has no need for those niceties. He attempts to pick up a pancake and succeeds only in tearing off a piece. No matter. He conveys it to his mouth and begins to chew.

Adam is transported. He has never tasted anything like this pancake. All that has ever passed his lips was bland and tasteless manna. His knees sag, and he nearly faints from the overwhelming pleasures assaulting his mouth, his palate, his taste buds, his papillae, his nostrils. The combined taste of sugar and salt is ecstasy. The grainy texture of the cake as it coats his tongue is inconceivably delicious. He revels in the experience of the warm food coursing down his gullet. Never has his stomach experienced such delight. He tears off another piece and consumes it greedily. He quickly finishes his plate, moaning in pleasure with every bite. Adam's head is spinning. So much has happened in the last few hours: the discovery of other members of his species; of solo bicycles; of *Ragbray*; of elephant-sized bicycles; of hills, indexed shifting, shift levers in the brakes, freewheeling, clothes, water bottles, sunglasses. And now pancakes. Adam is slowly getting this figured out. That's good; he likes to solve problems. But the incredible pancakes lying warm in his stomach, the strain of the morning's hills, the low oxygen content of the air and the stress on his limited problem-solving abilities make Adam drowsy. He finds a spot among the cyclists sitting against the side of the fire house. His head begins to nod and he falls asleep, the empty paper plate still in his hand.

CHAPTER TEN

I saw somewhere that the practice of using bicycle riders as messengers probably had its start in the 1870s, when some French newspaper hired guys on bikes to carry information from Paris to Versailles—about 15 miles. They rode either velocipedes—the old boneshakers—or the new English-style high-wheelers, and were expected to make the trip in about an hour. Fifteen miles in an hour would have been easy for the high-wheelers, but I bet the guys on the boneshakers really had to hump! They also used bike couriers to carry information from the Paris stock exchange to some telegraph site six miles away. By the turn of the twentieth century postmen delivering mail and cops covering their beats were using two-wheeled machines. Bicycles, tricycles, and even quadricycles were used by deliverymen of various sorts to transport groceries, produce, and goods of all kinds. Bulky items too large to carry on the machine itself were towed behind, in large, wheeled cargo boxes. Knife and scissor sharpeners hauled their grindstones with their tricycles. In 1909 the Pope Manufacturing Company began building machines specifically designed for the delivery market. There were other makers too, all turning out strong, heavy-duty bicycles built to withstand a lot of punishment.

The bicycle turned out to be a great tool of commerce. It cost less than a horse and required practically no upkeep. It didn't shit in the streets, either, and believe me, that was no small thing. Of course, when the automobile came along it swept away the practical appeal of the bike. Also, after World War I, cars and trucks became increasingly affordable, and there's no denying that a light truck could carry a lot more payload than a bike. Still, tough, heavy-duty bicycles and tricycles could carry lots of goods on built-in front and rear racks, and these brutes never went completely out of favor. They're still heavily utilized in the less industrialized parts of the world. One popular incarnation of this machine, the rickshaw, or pedicab, is designed to transport human cargo. They even have them in New York now.

Around the beginning of the twentieth century Western Union started using boys as bicycle messengers. For more than 50 years it was a great thing for a kid to do—it was supposed to build character! But not any more—hell, there aren't even any telegrams any more. Kids used to use bikes to deliver newspapers, too; being a newsboy was another job that was supposed to build character. It taught you to be a junior businessman. But like the Western Union messenger, the newsboy is no more. Now newspapers are delivered by adult businessmen, in cars.

Bicycle couriers have been around now for more than a century. The concept began to make sense with the dual development of fast, safe bicycles and smooth city roads; but it wasn't until after the Second World War that messengers became a fixture on the streets of New York City. With more than 5,000 professional riders out and about on Manhattan Island, you're bound to spot one of us within minutes of stepping out of a subway station. Typically, we'll be racing through the streets with seemingly little regard for pedestrians or automobiles. With our bags or backpacks slung over our shoulders, radio, cell phone, and maybe an iPod clipped to the strap, we'll be riding flat out, hell-bent on reaching our destination. We might be carrying theater tickets, legal papers, court documents, contracts, packages, food, clothing, jewelry, medical supplies, blood, body parts, or for all we know, contraband or explosives; but our mission is to get the cargo delivered and signed for at the soonest possible moment, so that we can fly to the next pick-up point and begin the game over again.

By the 1980s bike messengering had achieved a certain panache. The dangers involved in all-day street riding, the lack of job security and insurance, and the low pay scale, combined with the dashing figure of the flying cyclist, the lawlessness of riding up one-way streets and cruising through stop lights, the trendy clothes, the fancy helmets, the crazy hair styles, the body piercings, the fly-boy sunglasses, the mysterious shoulder bags, and the up-yours attitude, transformed those couriers into the new sex symbol of the youth culture. The popular picture of the messenger was undoubtedly influenced by the rise of the office cubical and the beginnings of the widespread use of computers in business. In a way, messengering became a revolt against the nine-to-five life spent staring at a monitor, hemmed in by the three sides of a constraining box. The bike courier sent out a message: "I am not a drone. I do not slave in a cubical like you thousands of worker bees. I am free. I am independent. I go where I want, when I want, and how I want." As usual, reality differs from fantasy.

Bike messengers come in all flavors. While the statistics are dominated by young Caucasian males, there are a significant number of African Americans, Asians, Puerto Ricans, and women. The typical courier may be a jock, but there are plenty of tree huggers, granola munchers, and middle-aged laborer types plying the pedals in the streets. What we all share is a love for cycling, a dislike of supervision, and a loathing for cubical life. And we're all physically fit—I mean, really fit. You cannot be a messenger if you're not; you just won't make it past the first few days. And those who do make it will tell you that although they thought they were in great shape, it took them a few weeks before they could come home at the end of the day without their legs, arms, and backs aching from the strain of eight hours or more in the saddle, day in and day out.

Strangely, most couriers consider what they're doing as fun rather than work; and for many, that's the problem. Being a messenger gives them a chance to play with their toys all day. I've heard people say that bicycle messengering is nothing more than a way of prolonging childhood. Eventually, they say, those guys and gals need to grow up and find out what it is they'll do for the rest of their lives; that while most of the population are finding out how the real world works, messengers are just putting that day off. They say that making less money than you're capable of is admirable if you're doing it for a genuine cause; but it doesn't make much sense if you're doing it simply to postpone adulthood. But try telling that to a messenger.

CHAPTER ELEVEN

Adam wakes up to find Eve anxiously hovering over him. The long-absent snake is lounging a few feet away, a contented smile on his face. Incongruously, he is wearing tiny sunglasses over his beady eyes.

"Adam, are you OK?" asks Eve. "You were moaning in your sleep."

Adam sits up and looks around, confused and dazed. It is not midday, it is early morning. There is no firehouse, no firemen, no line of griddles, no pancakes. Jack is gone. His fellow *Ragbray* bicyclists are gone. He is back in the old part of Eden, his Eden. He did not understand how he was transported to the Iowa part, and now he cannot understand how he has been transported back to familiar territory. He looks down at his wrist to double check, but the grey band is gone.

"Eve," he says groggily, as he gets to his feet, "I was in this place called *Eye-oh-wa*. I was on County Road *dee thirty ate*, on a *Ragbray* bicycle ride. I was riding a strange kind of bicycle, half a tandem, for one person only, a solo bike. The Garden was gone. There was no jungle, no curving macadam. Instead, the path went straight ahead, as far as you could see. There were fields of tall plants and low leafy vegetation and animals I'd never seen before, and weird-looking enormous white boxes." Adam is recovering his senses and is really getting wound up.

"But strangest of all there were lots and lots of species members just like you and me. Some were riding tandems, but most were on solo bicycles wearing different-colored clothes and naked arms and legs and there were hills and water in bottles and Jack showed me how to change gears in the brake levers with indexed shifting and there were elephant bicycles that smelled and burning flesh and I ate pancakes and it is the most wonderful manna I ever tasted. But I don't know how I got there. I don't know how I got back here."

Eve has no idea what he's talking about, but the wily boa does. He comes closer to the pair.

"You had a dream, Adam," he hisses, barely able to contain his delight.

"A dream? What do you mean, a dream? What is a dream?"

"A dream is an imaginary series of thoughts, images, and experiences you have while you're sleeping," explains the snake. Some explanation! Adam doesn't understand a word.

"But why was he moaning?" asks a concerned Eve.

"Uh"—Adam gets it now—"I was moaning because the pancakes tasted so good," he remembers with pleasure.

"But if they were so good why did they make you moan? And what is pancakes?" she presses.

"Eve, the pancakes looked like large, flat cakes of manna but they tasted nothing like manna." Adam tries to describe a pancake by surrounding the air with his thumbs and forefingers. "The smell was incredible and the flavors exploded in my mouth. The delicious textures coated my tongue. And after I ate them the pancakes warmed my stomach."

Adam pats his abdomen. "That's why I was moaning—they were so good. It's impossible to describe them. I can still taste them."

Eve is completely mystified by Adam's explanation, but dream or no, it is time for breakfast. Over their morning manna, which, given his new-found love of pancakes, he can scarcely bring himself to eat, Adam gives Eve and the snake a detailed account of the dream. He remembers every bit of it. It is, after all, the only dream he has ever had. He describes in detail the large, smooth road surface with its painted lines, the grassy ditches, the waving fields of corn, the broad expanses of leafy soy beans, the lethargic cattle, the grazing sheep, the scurrying pigs, the effects of the oxygen-poor atmosphere, the odor of the fertilizer, the telephone poles lining the road, the passing cars, the houses, barns, outbuildings, trailers, trucks, and pickups he saw, the food vendors at the sides of the road, all so unlike the verdant and colorful jungle of the Eden they know. He tells Eve that the two of them are not alone in Eden; that there is an *Eye-oh-wa* part, where they ride the *Ragbray* on County Road *dee thirty ate*, and where there are a seemingly unlimited supply of species members, almost all on bicycles, and all wearing colorful skin coverings called clothes. He describes his conversations with Jack, his discovery of the wonders of indexed shifting, his mastery of shifters in the brake levers, how he conquered hill climbing, and how he came to discover pancakes.

"I drank water from a vessel," he tells them. "It was called a 'bottle.' You have to pull it open with your teeth and squeeze it with your hand to make the water come out. It wasn't like the water in this part of Eden—it had a funny taste to it. But here's the thing: in order to get the bottle I had to let go of one of the handlebars and reach down, like this."

Adam accompanies his recitation with a graphic enactment. "I was squeezing the bottle and drinking water with one hand and steering with the other. At first I was afraid, but it was easy!"

Eve is fascinated, and her eyes glow with admiration as Adam describes how bit by bit he came to make sense of the strange and different land. "Adam is clever and strong," she thinks to herself. "He is a real problem solver."

"Almost all the other species members wore dark circle things over their eyes. Jack called them 'sunglasses.' I don't understand how they were able to see the road and not bump into each other with their eyes covered like that, but they didn't seem to have any trouble. And the macadam had a smooth black surface on it. It was easy to ride on, except when I was going up a hill. I don't like hills. They're hard to go up and when you come down you have to stop pedaling or you're going to be in trouble. I'm glad we don't have any hills in this part of Eden."

The reptile listens silently, his forked tongue flicking in and out, a crafty smile on his thin lips. Adam is still uncertain about the mechanism of the event and cannot believe that his experience was not real. In fact, it is still so real that he doesn't even comment on the fact that the boa is wearing sunglasses. But he turns to him for an explanation.

"What is this *Ragbray* ride I was on?" he queries the serpent.

"It's a bicycle ride across Iowa. It takes place every year and it's sponsored by the *Des Moines Register*. It's called RAGBRAI, which means the 'Register's Annual Great Bike Ride Across Iowa'."

Another non-answer from the snake. "What is the _Dee-moyn Register?_"

"It's a newspaper in Iowa."

This is getting Adam nowhere. He decides to take another tack.

74

"Why are you wearing those dark circles—ah, sunglasses—in front of your eyes?"

"They protect my eyes from the sun."

"But you can't see anything through them."

"It just seems that way. I can see just fine, and I don't have to squint."

"Was I actually in the *Eye-oh-wa* part of Eden?"

"No, you weren't. You were still in Eden. Besides, Iowa isn't in Eden."

"That's what Jack said. But how could I be here and there at the same time?"

"You just were. That's why it's called a dream."

"How come I never dreamed before?"

"You never had anything to dream about."

"Do you dream?"

"All the time."

"Does Eve dream?"

"Not yet."

"Does the lion dream? How about the giraffe?"

"The lion and the giraffe are animals, dumb beasts. They don't dream."

"Does God dream?"

"You *are* God's dream!" says the gleeful boa over his shoulder, as he glides back into the jungle. As usual, the naïve couple have to be satisfied with the snake's tantalizing answers. But dream or no, it is time for them to begin the day's circumnavigation. As they mount their tandem Adam tells Eve,

"Water bottles, sunglasses, clothes, pancakes, indexed shifting—now we have lots of things to ask God for."

CHAPTER TWELVE

Public roads were fairly primitive before the early part of the nineteenth century. Most, like those in England, consisted of little more than rutted dirt and gravel paths, many of them decaying survivors from the days of the Roman occupation. In fair weather they provided an adequate navigable surface for slow, horse-drawn traffic; but with rain and melting snow they turned to muddy quagmires, making progress even slower and sometimes impossible. The institution of the turnpike trust was an important attempt to better these roads, and between 1750 and 1825 there were more than 1,000 of them operating in Great Britain. The trusts were set up to collect tolls from the horse-drawn traffic, with the revenues applied to the maintenance and improvement of the roads under their control. Although there were no generally accepted standards, roads were often upgraded by providing a foundation of large stones with smaller rocks on top, cambered in cross section so that water would run off to the sides. It was left for the traffic to compact the surface.

John McAdam, the Scottish engineer who was appointed surveyer of the Bristol turnpike in 1816, improved on this system. First, he specified that ditches be dug along the sides of the road bed. A layer of subsoil was laid down, then a base of large stones, arranged to form a camber. Over this was placed 10 inches of crushed rock—McAdam specified that each weigh no more than six ounces and be no larger than an egg—and the whole was bound with gravel. These layers were then sprayed with water and compacted with heavy cast-iron horse-drawn rollers. The result, first applied to the 175 miles of thoroughfare that made up the Bristol turnpike, was a hard, smooth, elevated road with a surface impervious to water. Rain and melting snow effectively drained off its crowned surface to the ditches on either side. The paved surface of roads so constructed was called "macadam," and the procedure was known as "macadamization." The process revolutionized transportation, for the first time providing fast, safe, smooth roads. By the end of the nineteenth century macadamization had spread all over Europe, then to America and the rest of the world. The system has influenced road-building ever since.

America was slow to adopt macadamization, but the process was considerably encouraged in the 1880s by the formation of a national bicycling organization, the "League of American Wheelmen" (now known as the "League of American Bicyclists"). One of its first acts was to initiate the Good Roads Movement, in which bicyclists by the thousands involved themselves in local and national politics, organized conventions and demonstrations, wrote pamphlets describing the benefits of good roads, and threw their support behind local politicians who supported their cause. The bicycle thus became the primary driving force behind the development of macadamized roads in the United States. The first true bicycle boom, a veritable explosion of two-wheelers in the early 1890s, when the safety bicycle with pneumatic tires became the dominant self-propelled machine, would not have been possible without the burgeoning road system already in place, and the development of the automobile only a few short years later would not have occurred so rapidly without the presence of macadamized roads. The automobile created a new problem, though: its weight and the speed of its tires' rotation destabilized the macadam, loosening and crushing the fine stone to a powder that was typically dissipated in clouds of dust. The difficulty was solved by binding the macadamized roads with tar or asphalt, thus transforming "macadam" into "tarmac."

CHAPTER THIRTEEN

"Then the eyes of both were opened, and they knew that they were naked. . ."
(Genesis 3:7)

"God! God! Adam here, Sir, with Eve. We'd like to talk to you."

Adam and Eve are standing in their clearing, facing the walnut tree, expecting it to burst into flames, as it did the last time they called on their Maker. But there are no flames; instead, there is the ominous sound of weighty footsteps. To the pair's amazement, a man comes striding out of the jungle. He is a big man, a very big man, approximately eight feet tall. His powerfully-built body radiates a life-giving force. There is a swirl of haze around his head, and with his heavily-bearded face, it is impossible to make out his features or even the color of his hair. He is wearing a flowing, full-length white cotton robe, and his feet are shod in well-worn leather sandals. A staff as tall as he is clenched in his right hand. The sight of the man is startling to Adam, but he recognizes the giant as a member of his species. He has, after all, seen other men, in his dream, even if not as large. Eve, on the other hand, grips Adam's arm, barely able to comprehend that she is seeing another human form.

"God? Are you God?" she gasps incredulously.

"Of course I am God," replies the apparition in a booming but not unpleasant voice. "Who do you think I am?"

"But you look so different this time. You're not a tree. And you're not on fire," says a relieved Eve, emboldened by God's relatively benign response.

"I am omnipotent. I can appear in any form I wish."

"But," says the confused Adam, "you're wearing. . . clothes." Adam recognizes that bicycling shorts, jerseys, and God's robe are all described by the term "clothes." He is proud to have made an intellectual leap.

"I told you," says God sharply, "I am omnipotent. I can wear anything I want. Like this."

In a flash of light the robe and sandals are gone, and God is wearing a grey, wool, three-piece business suit with a solid gold necktie. His french-cuffed cotton shirt, also grey, is adorned with ornate gold links. He is shod in gold lamé socks and brown leather oxfords. His left index finger is encircled by a large gold band, and the same digit on the opposite hand sports an enormous sparkling diamond. His severe face is framed by a luxurious mustache and a full Van Dyke beard. A gold homburg crowns his head of wavy dark hair. He is smoking a large cigar and he is wearing sunglasses. One foot is placed in front of the other and his arms are folded across his chest. As the awed pair gasp in disbelief, there is another flash and God is back in his robe and sandals, holding his staff.

"Now," says God crossly, addressing Adam, "how do you know about clothes? The snake told you, did he not?

"No," replies Adam, figuring he's one up on God this time. "I had a dream. I was on a solo bicycle on a ride called *Ragbray* in some part of Eden called *Eye-oh-wa*, on County Road *dee thirty ate*. There were lots and lots of other species members, all around me, riding bicycles. They were all wearing clothes and almost all of them had sunglasses in front of their eyes."

"How do you know it was a dream?" asks God.

"The snake told me," says Adam cautiously, knowing how God feels about the boa.

"Of course the snake told you," grumbles God. "Who else! He gave you that dream, you know."

"The snake gave me the dream?" says Adam in surprise. "I didn't know that! Why would he do that?"

"Listen, children," says God, not unkindly, but nevertheless evading the question. "The snake only appears to be your friend. But he is going to get you in deep trouble. We do not get along, the snake and I, and he is using you to get back at me."

"Why don't you get along?" The words pop out of Eve's mouth before she's had a chance to think. But God evades the question once again.

"Eve, my child, the snake is evil. He is out to destroy Eden and he is trying to do it by corrupting you and Adam. He gave Adam that dream, hoping you would ask me for more things."

This bit of news, though incomprehensible, is nevertheless distressing. Adam and Eve have no concept of good, so how can they understand evil? What is "corruption"? Furthermore, they recall that it was God, not the boa, who threatened to destroy Eden. And how bad could the snake be, if God created him? And if the snake really is that bad, why doesn't God make him not exist? God's answers, in other words, are as enigmatic as the snake's. But Adam catches one inference.

"Do you mean you don't want us to ask for things?" As if he didn't know. But the answer surprises him.

"I cannot stop you from asking for things," responds God. "That is the way I set things up and it would be too much of an effort to change it. All I can tell you is that it is not a good idea for you to do it. It is not a good idea at all."

Adam pushes on, nevertheless. "But we really need some bicycling clothes. I met this fellow Jack in my dream, and he told me that the clothes will protect our bodies from the sun, and the shorts have padding that will help keep our butts comfortable. Besides, he said it's not nice to ride without clothes. We'd like to have sunglasses, too. They'll protect our eyes from the sun."

God gives a weary sigh. "Adam, do you think I would create a sun that would damage you and Eve? Do you not realize that this Jack was a figment of the snake's imagination? Do you not realize that the boa directed that entire dream? But—if you must have clothes and sunglasses, so you shall."

With that God turns and strides back into the jungle.

Adam is jubilant, delighted to hear that his wishes will be fulfilled so easily. Eve is pleased that she and Adam have prevailed over God once again. God was so nice this time! He didn't yell or threaten, and he seemed to show genuine concern for their well-being. Maybe God is changing, they think. Still, where are the clothes and sunglasses? When they asked for shoes they appeared immediately, and helmets came right out of the tree; but this event is different. Soon it is time to retire, and thinking that God has reneged on his promise, the pair stretch out on the soft grass and fall into a disappointed sleep. When they awake at first light they discover two white cardboard boxes tied up in twine lying at their feet. The boa glides out of the jungle to find them seated cross-legged on the ground, examining the packages, frustration etched on their faces.

"Ah," he says delightedly, "you got your clothes and sunglasses."

"No," replies Eve, "we found these. . .these things, what ever they are."

"Boxes. Those 'things' are boxes, tied up in twine, and your stuff is inside them."

"But how do we get them out?" asks Adam, puzzled.

In reply, the serpent scours the ground with his beady eyes.

"Pick up that sharp stone," he tells Adam, pointing with his long tongue." Adam complies.

"Now rub it against the twine."

Adam does as he suggests, and goes to work on his box. After some vigorous sawing the twine parts. The snake slithers over, hooks one of his fangs under the box's cover and flips it open. To the amazement and delight of Adam and Eve, a pair of sunglasses with black frames and brown-tinted lenses is revealed. The heavy temples sport a "Gucci" logo. The eyewear is sitting on top of a red and grey Pearl Izumi short-sleeve jersey and a pair of black Cannondale bicycling shorts, both in Adam's size. Adam removes the items from the container as Eve, following suit, quickly saws through her twine. Her box contains the same items, identical except for size. The pair are bewildered by the zippers on their jerseys, but the snake shows them how to open and close them. Little cardboard folders with indecipherable markings are hanging off the garments, held by plastic loops. Adam, proving himself to be a thorough-going techno-whiz, saws through the loops with the sharp stone. With the empty boxes, the sawed-up twine, and the cardboard folders, for the first time Eden has a waste problem; but it is of little concern to the pair, who simply toss it all into the underbrush.

It is nearly time to get underway, so they quickly eat their manna, and with the assistance of the snake, don their new apparel. The jerseys have three large pockets in the back for various accoutrements, and mesh panels along the sides to admit air. Had they been able to decipher the marks on the cardboard folders they would have discovered that the shirts are made from a material that wicks perspiration away from the body. The shorts, made from a smooth fabric and expertly sewn together from eight individual panels, and with gel pads in the crotch, fit them like second skins. When they add their shoes, sunglasses, and helmets, the snake tells them they look absolutely resplendent. Adam is filled with pride. He could now be in the *Ragbray* and he'd look just like everyone else. The clothes are restraining and uncomfortable, but now that he has them Adam is determined to wear them. The sunglasses are strange, but in the bright sunlight the effect is not unpleasant. Eve complains that the shorts bind her crotch, but Adam tells her that she has no choice, that the clothes have come from God and he would be insulted if she didn't wear them. Furthermore, he says, they need the protection from the sun.

The pair begin the day's circumnavigation. Although bicycling in clothing feels peculiar, they quickly become accustomed to it. Besides, the padding between the saddle and the butt feels good. But Eden has changed again. Before they cover much distance at all Adam sees a mild hill in front of him. Hills in Eden! Hills have never been here before! Bewildered, he checks himself: is he back in *Eye-oh-wa*, on the *Ragbray*, dreaming once again? No, he is riding the old familiar tandem, and Eve is sitting behind him, chattering on about the benefits of sunglasses. Warned that they are approaching a hill, she looks around Adam's broad back to view the phenomenon for herself. To see the macadam heading in an upward direction, even a little, is unsettling. But Adam, with his new-found mastery of gears, manages the slight rise with aplomb, easily making the connection between the manner in which he operated the indexed shifters in the brake levers of his solo dream machine, and controlling the friction shifters on the tandem's down tube. Eve conveys to Adam her admiration of his shifting skills, and they tell each other that there is actually a certain enjoyment in traversing the hill. The downshifting on the upside, the freewheeling on the downside—these are things they do not normally do. The hill has introduced a little variety into their daily routine, and although they cannot imagine how it got there, they decide that their circumnavigations were rather monotonous before the hill came into their lives.

Soon, however, they encounter another hill, then another, and another, not all of them as mild as the first. They pass the lion, who is as confused as the cyclists about the transformation in the terrain. He tilts his head one way as the tandem ascends the hill in front of him, and the other way as they descend, attempting to see the riders on their usual level plane. Ordinarily the lion would be unconcerned and dismiss the anomaly from his placid mind; but today it disturbs him. Today he does not like this variation from established norm. It agitates him. His blood quickens, and he experiences a pressure in his head and a hollow under his ribs. The discomfort can only be assuaged by dashing after the tandem, by doing something to the riders—he knows not what—that would teach them not to upset his orderly world. He begins to rise, but the moment passes before he reaches the macadam. He crouches back down and resolves the issue by emitting an ear-splitting roar.

Hill-climbing is hard on the quadriceps, and by the time they dismount for their midday manna Adam and Eve's legs are sore. Because of the wicking qualities of their bicycling jerseys they find themselves less sweaty than usual, but they are hotter and thirstier than they have ever been at high sun. They drink thirstily from the cool stream before eating, agreeing that their love for the novelty of hills may have been misplaced. The afternoon's ride is no better, and the pair are weary and aching by the time they return home. Once again, although they still do not realize it, the days have gotten longer in Eden.

They eat their manna cakes and prepare for a quick bath in the stream. Eve raised her arms and pulls her jersey off over her head. Without premeditation Adam observes Eve's soft, shapely breasts and pink nipples as they emerge from her clothing and is charmed by the sight. He has gazed at those apple-like globes every day since the beginning of creation, but he has never before noticed their allure in this way. He experiences a sensation of delight and warmth as his eyes slide over the form of his lovely and vivacious partner. But then he feels the blood rush to his face, and a tingling sensation emanates from his groin and spreads over his body. Suddenly his bicycling shorts are too tight, and he tugs the restraining garment off his body. He looks up to see Eve staring at his crotch. "What is she looking at?" he wonders. He peers down himself and is amazed to see his penis standing out from his body, as proud and stiff as a young tree trunk. Eve's eyes widen and her nipples stiffen as she sees that Adam's familiar and normally unremarkable phallus has grown to twice its usual size and assumed a horizontal position. She drinks in Adam's magnificent physique and thinks to herself, "He is my Adam. He is beautiful, and his wondrously stiff penis is a thing of splendor. Adam is like a God." Her vulva unexpectedly feels odd and her body flushes. Her vagina feels like it is turning to water. In fact, Adam and Eve are in the early stages of sexual arousal and their genitalia are coursing with their hot blood. They are confused, their minds are whirling, and they are asking themselves why the sight of the other's familiar body should have this unexpectedly strange effect on them. Finally, the moment passes. A cool soak in the stream calms them physically, leaving them only with their baffled emotions. Exhausted, they lie down and fall into their usual deep sleep.

CHAPTER FOURTEEN

Routing is one of the most important elements of a messenger's job, and it's one over which I have little control. My dispatcher decides where and how far I go to make a pickup and a delivery, and since my salary depends on commissions, it's my dispatcher who decides how much money I'll make at the end of the day. Sure, there are tips, but they're rare, since most of my deliveries are to secretaries and receptionists. No—I make my money on the number of deliveries I can manage. Urgent deliveries pay more, and a good dispatcher will spread those around, like handing out candy canes at Christmas. When you're a rookie, nothing but a new number, you'll find that you're knocking yourself out making ordinary deliveries and you'll come home with a pretty flimsy paycheck, while the guys and gals who are tight with the dispatcher get the emergency calls and make twice as much as you with half the work. So it pays to get along with your dispatcher!

If your routing is always shitty your dispatcher probably has it in for you, and probably the best thing to do is quit and go to work for another company. There are dozens of courier businesses in New York, and any one of them will hire a messenger with some experience. In fact, that's something of an incentive for your dispatcher to treat you decently. She knows that if she doesn't, you can up and quit and be working for a rival company tomorrow, and then she'll either be shorthanded or have to take the time to break in a new courier. But it also pays for you to keep a cool head about it. Don't get pissed off when you get some bad routing, because that distracts you from *the* most important part of your job, riding safely. That means you wear a helmet all the time and keep your brakes, tires, and drive train in first-class shape; but it also means that you accept some bad routing as part of the job.

You're not going to make much of a salary when you're a rookie, no matter how you're routed. You don't know the streets, the shortcuts, the alleys, the lights, the traffic patterns, the bus routes, the construction sites, the one-ways and the thousands of other things that get you quickly from point A to point B, so your delivery times will be a lot longer than they will once you learn the territory. You'll start out making not much more than minimum wage. Your weekly check will increase to maybe double that, but that's about as high as it's going to go, and when things are slow that income is going to dip and there's not much you can do about it.

One of the benefits of messengering is the increase in your fitness level. You'll have to be fit to begin with, otherwise you won't last a week; but you'll find that riding that bike eight to 10 hours a day, day in and day out, is going to take some weight off you. I lost 10 pounds in my first month as a courier, and I sleep like a baby every night. I feel better, my body is tight, strong, and toned, and I have an appetite like a horse. For a while I had a sense of well-being like I'd never experienced before, but after I reached that peak I started to think about other things, mostly like how dangerous this job is. The fear of getting hit by a car, or getting wiped out by a jay walker, or collecting a door prize grows on you, day after day, and you realize that the law of averages is going to catch up to you sooner or later.

I've been in a couple of pretty good accidents since I started messengering. I've had frames bent and wheels destroyed, and I had one really close call when I nearly got crushed between a truck and a parked car. But fortunately, I've never been seriously injured. You hope to get out of the game before that happens, but it seems that just about every day you hear of someone you know getting into some kind of trouble.

Still, the lure of messengering is what keeps us all on the job. I'm my own boss. There's no one staring down my neck all day. My dispatcher doesn't care what I do, as long as the package gets delivered on time. If I want to goof off and stop for a cup of coffee there's no one to tell me I'm wasting company time. And I have to admit it—there's something sexy about messengering. People think you're a different breed—that you have some outlaw blood in your veins. They're jealous, wishing they could exchange their cubicles for your life of freedom. They admire your derring-do, your clothes, your bike, your bag, and the dangers you face every day on the streets of New York. If you're not too scruffy and don't have any visible tattoos you can often pick up some of the hot young women who populate New York offices. I've had my share of girls who were fascinated by my anti-establishment image.

Strangely enough, you develop casual relationships with others who work in the streets. After a while you come to recognize the mailmen, the FedEx and UPS delivery guys, and the people selling ice cream, roasted chestnuts, hot dogs, and gyros. A bond develops between you and them, and you'll wave, nod, or lift a hand off the handlebars in silent greeting when your paths cross. The connection is this: we don't work in an office and we don't work for a boss; we may be out in the cold or the heat, or the snow, or the rain, but we answer to no one; we're tough, superior to the rest of the hot-house population commuting to their 9 to 5 jobs, with someone artificially controlling the temperature and humidity in their cubicles. Only the hardiest survive in the streets of New York, and we're among them.

You also develop an affection for the city itself. I love riding through Central Park on an autumn day, or checking out the gawkers on the steps of the Metropolitan Museum. Even the busy cross-town streets get my grudging admiration, the way they throw up one obstacle after another. Nothing brings me more joy than beating the lights and the vehicle traffic, going four or five blocks across town. A car insulates you from the world outside, but when you're on a bike you're part of that world. The down-side is that when you get home at night your skin is filthy from a combination of exhaust fumes and road grime. I guess the whole thing is a trade off.

CHAPTER FIFTEEN

It is the middle of the night. A full moon and a sky glistening with bright, hard, starry points illuminate the clearing where Adam and Eve are asleep. The pale light reveals the snake, who glides silently out of the jungle and lightly drapes his body over the dormant Eve's abdomen. The tip of his prehensile tail creeps to her crotch, burrows in her pubic hair, parts her labia, and finds her clitoris. The boa begins a gentle, rhythmic massage of that sensual organ, every once in a while sliding down to dip into her vagina. Soon his phallic-like appendage is glistening in the moonlight, coated with Eve's warm and slippery emissions. His forked tongue flicks in and out of his thin lips as he throws his narrow head back in delight. His tail keeps up its pulsing dance, probing deeper into the sleeper's warm, wet orifice. Murmuring with inchoate pleasure, Eve begins to thrash around, her body feverish, her breath now coming in quick, shallow spurts. She appears to be on the verge of either waking or experiencing an orgasm—perhaps both—and neither suits the intruding reptile's purpose. He removes his tail and waits for the disturbed young woman to settle down. In time, Eve returns to a deep sleep. Satisfied, the snake silently glides back into the jungle.

As usual, the pair awake at first light. Eve is troubled. She rolls over to Adam.

"Adam, I had a dream last night—at least I think it was a dream."

Adam is all ears. He is, after all, the resident expert on dreams.

"Were you riding a bicycle in *Eye-oh-wa?*" he asks. "Were you on a *Ragbray?* Were you on County Road *dee thirty ate?*"

"No, it was nothing like that. There was something playing around my vagina. Then it went *into* my vagina, in and out, in and out. It was so strange. And the strangest part is that I liked it. It really felt good. It made me feel wonderful—it made my whole body feel wonderful—and at the same time it was disturbing. Very disturbing. I was upset and I don't know why. It made me want something, but I don't know what it was. It left me unsatisfied. When I woke up there was nothing there. Nothing."

Adam is disappointed. "That's all? No *Ragbray*? No solo bicycle?"

"No, no, it had nothing to do with bicycles or riding. It was all about my vagina."

Adam is nonplused. What sort of dream is this? He knows all about *Ragbrays* and bicycles and gears, but Eve's vagina is a closed book to him. As far as he knows, that's where she passes water, and he doesn't see why dreaming about that should cause any excitement. But then he has an epiphany: after all, his penis is where *he* passes water, and *it* was certainly feeling strange yesterday evening, when it unexpectedly stiffened and grew. In fact, it was sort of like Eve said—wonderful and disturbing at the same time, and it affected his entire body. There was an unknown and unsatisfied desire there, too.

Adam shares his insight with Eve, but it explains nothing. They have no concept of sexuality. They do not know the word and if they did, they would not know what it meant. Procreation is unknown to them, and at any rate, unnecessary in Eden, which was designed to operate without sexual intercourse. Like speech, God has given Adam and Eve sexuality, but does not want them to know about it. God certainly does not want them to *do* it. God should have known better.

Neither youth understands what is happening, so they wait for the snake to appear. The snake will explain it to them, even if they don't understand his explanation. But today the snake does not appear.

CHAPTER SIXTEEN

The velocipede craze is at its peak in France, and Pierre Michaux's factory cannot turn out units fast enough to satisfy the demand. So in 1868 the inventor-cum-industrialist crosses the channel to Coventry, England, and licenses the Coventry Sewing Machine Company to build his machines for the French market. But timing is everything. The Franco-Prussian war intervenes two years later, and the French market for bicycles vanishes. The Coventry Company, now awash in velocipedes, is forced to sell its production at home, in England.

Enter James Starley, one of the owners of the sewing machine company and a true mechanical genius. Starley was intrigued by the concept of the boneshaker, but looked on Michaux's primitive mechanism with some disdain. He set out to convert the heavy, lumbering velocipede into a light, fast, reliable, self-propelled vehicle, and he succeeded beyond anyone's expectations. His first design was the "Coventry," a lighter machine than the boneshaker, with the saddle brought close to the top of the front wheel to provide the rider with more favorable pedaling leverage. Although the Coventry was a great improvement over the boneshaker, Starley's real triumph, the 1870 "Ariel," was even lighter in weight, and increased the diameter of the front wheel from an already large 35 inches to an enormous 48. Significantly, the saddle was placed directly over the bicycle's center of gravity, assuring the rider a pedaling position of maximum efficiency. Starley's new self-propelled vehicle, dubbed the "high wheeler," was light-years ahead of the velocipede. And it was one of the strangest devices for personal transportation ever seen on the planet.

The reasoning behind the development of the high wheeler was impeccable: since bicycles were still crank-driven from the front wheel, like the present-day child's tricycle (a direct descendent of the boneshaker), it was clear that the larger the wheel the more ground one could cover with one revolution of the pedals. With advances in wire-wheel design, front wheels quickly grew to diameters of up to 50 and even 60 inches (front wheel dimensions were not standard; rather, the size purchased depended on the length of the rider's legs as well as his sense of derring-do), while rear wheels shrank to something like 16 inches. Solid rubber tires became standard equipment, and improvements in metallurgy, allowing the use of tubular frames and lighter components, helped reduce the weight of the machines to something like 40 pounds.

Because the disparity in size between front and rear wheels was similar to that of penny and farthing coins, the nickname "penny farthing" became a familiar and somewhat pejorative term for the high wheeler. Later, when so-called safety bicycles became more common, the high wheeler was called the "ordinary," since by then it was regarded as the ordinary form of the machine, as opposed to all others.

Starley's new breed of bicycle had many positive qualities. The rider sat high in the air, his head elevated by as much as eight feet above the road dust, majestically surveying the surrounding countryside. The enormous front wheel, with its rubber tires and bearings much improved over those in the old boneshakers, soaked up the bumps and shocks of uneven road surfaces like a piston in an oil bath. Steering and braking were more positive, and the steel frames were thinner and lighter. These machines were far more advanced than velocipedes, and they were *fast*. Speed records were established and broken with regularity. Sprinting racers were able to maintain a scorching pace of close to 20 miles an hour, while touring cyclists easily covered 70, 100, and even 200 miles in a day's ride. All in all, Starley's high wheeler was an enormous improvement over the old boneshaker.

But Starley's high wheeler had some major drawbacks. For one thing, simply mounting and dismounting the machine presented major difficulties. As awkward as it was to get on or off a velocipede, it was even more complicated on a high wheeler. It was virtually impossible to vault into the shoulder-height saddle from a running start, so a small step was mounted over the rear wheel. The rider now had two choices: either run alongside the machine and, once minimum velocity had been attained, get one foot up on the step and from there propel himself into the saddle; or, from a standing start, put one foot on the step, push off with the other, then climb into the saddle. In either case, once seated the rider's feet then had to find and engage the pedals, whose continually-rotating cranks were fixed to the wheel bearings. The routine was reversed when stopping. Either method was challenging, and effectively served to bar those not athletically gifted from cycling. It certainly barred women, with their long skirts.

A second disadvantage was more serious. As brilliant as the design was, it was also fundamentally dangerous. With the rider over the center of the enormous front wheel the machine was badly balanced front to rear, and when encountering any sort of obstruction, or even when braked too vigorously, it had an alarming tendency to tip forward and pitch the rider over the handlebars. "Taking a header" occurred with great regularity. Injuries were common and occasionally serious. Many strategies were invented to prevent headers, including the 1881 "American Star," which reversed the wheels, with the large one in the back and steering transferred to the smaller in front. Still, the threat was so great that some machines were made with handlebars that went under the legs, so that in the event of a header the rider could at least attempt to slide over the wheel and land on his feet. In fact, the more courageous or foolhardy riders developed the practice of putting their legs over the handlebars when coasting down hill (the legs had to go somewhere, since the cranks did not freewheel). This ostensibly decreased the risk of serious injury in case of a spill, since the rider's legs would not be trapped by the bars; but it further unbalanced the bicycle and increased the chance that the header would occur.

One would think that the precarious nature of the high wheeler would have deterred potential riders. Not at all! The imminent danger of being thrown over the front wheel only added to the panache of riding a high wheeler, and riding these machines was all about style!

Racing was popular, with thousands turning out to watch the daredevils propel their towering contraptions at breakneck speeds and perform feats of bicycling acrobatics. The gentry, on the other hand, organized themselves into exclusive riding clubs and undertook centuries and other long-distance outings. With strict dress codes, uniforms, dues, and rules, there was a strong element of class prejudice in the clubs and in bicycle ownership in general. It was young, elitist, upper-class, long-legged, athletic men who owned and rode these glamorous but dangerous machines, and those in the trades were simply barred from club membership. At any rate, the high wheeler found little favor with common workers, those who might have benefited most from a cheap, practical, and reliable self-propelled vehicle. That part of the population either continued to ride the slower, heavier, but safer velocipedes, now readily available on the second-hand market, or they rode minimally-large high wheelers, or tricycles, or they eschewed cycling altogether. Nevertheless, by the end of the decade of the 1880s more than 100,000 penny farthings had been produced by English makers. After the French bicycle industry recovered from the devastation of the Franco-Prussian war, it too switched to the new, dramatically faster English-style machine. Racing and touring made rapid post-war comebacks, now with high wheelers, and France regained a central position in bicycle manufacturing on the continent. The high wheeler quickly spread to Britain's colonies, to the rest of Europe, to the Far East, and to the New World.

After seeing the machine exhibited at the 1876 Centennial Exposition in Philadelphia, the Boston industrialist Albert A. Pope began importing high wheelers from England for sale in the United States. But Pope quickly realized that he could make more money by manufacturing them himself, so as Pierre Michaux had done a decade earlier, he turned to a sewing machine company. In 1879 he and his bicycle took a train to Hartford, Connecticut where, to the surprise and delight of the local citizenry, he rode his own Coventry-made "Duplex Excelsior" down the road from the railroad station to the Weed Sewing Machine Company. Since Weed's business was down it was not difficult to convince the manufacturer to take on the task of producing the bicycle, which Pope called the "Columbia" model. With that contract in his pocket, Pope had positioned himself to become known as the father of the modern bicycle.

Meanwhile, in a bizarre case of *déjà vu*, the issue of patent rights once again reared its head. Calvin Witty still owned the Lallement velocipede patent, and as he did in the late 1860s, he charged a hefty fee for every bicycle Pope produced. Pope was too clever for Witty, however, and with some wily maneuvering managed to acquire sole ownership of the patent. With the path now clear, Pope hoped to rejuvenate the American bicycle market. But America, with unhappy memories of its short-lived velocipede craze, was not clamoring for machines that would once again threaten pedestrians and frighten horses. And as superior as the high wheeler was to the old velocipede, the wretched condition of American roads still did not offer surfaces conducive to cycling. Nevertheless, the alluring penny farthing made some inroads, particularly when students in the Ivy League colleges began to form cycling clubs. Also, women became involved in racing almost immediately, and although some of them were first-class athletes, there is little doubt that to male spectators much of the racers' appeal was found in their scanty riding apparel. By 1879, with the wild success of six-day bicycle racing, it became clear that cycling was no longer merely a fad in North America. By 1890 the Columbia bicycle had done so well that it took over the entire Weed plant, producing some 60,000 units a year. Albert Pope was now the largest bicycle manufacturer in the world.

Pope was an indefatigable champion of his machine. He fought against the numerous anti-bicycle laws dating back to the days of the velocipede. He fostered the formation of the influential "League of American Wheelmen," whose elite membership pressed for better roadways. With his own money he financed the teaching of road engineering at the Massachusetts Institute of Technology. He sponsored publications dedicated to good roads. He lobbied state and federal officials in the cause of road improvement. His efforts gradually paid off, and by 1890 many federal and state road-building programs were in place, all in the service of the bicycle.

Until the end of the decade of the 1870s the tricycle had never seriously challenged the high wheeler. Other considerations aside, three wheelers took up more room, they were more complex, they took more power to propel, and they were certainly more expensive. Still, when

Queen Victoria started riding a Starley tricycle in 1881, they began to provide ordinaries with some real competition. A variety of three-wheeled machines appeared, offering safe alternatives to the penny farthing and affording transportation to doctors, merchants, older citizens, women, and those not athletically inclined. The Starley name was in the forefront again, with the "Coventry Rotary Tricycle," produced in 1878 by James' son Matthew and his nephew John. This strange-looking two-track machine had a large wheel on the left side of the rider and two smaller in-line wheels on the right. The cyclist turned pedals that drove the large wheel by means of a drive chain. The importance of this machine was not so much in its abilities as a self-propelled vehicle, but in its use of the chain. This device was not new, since there were instances of its application to velocipedes; but the quality of the chains available at that time had been poor, and nothing came of those earlier experiments. With improvements in metallurgy and design, however, the new-style chains easily proved their merit. Another development that came out of the tricycle was the differential gear, which allowed the large drive wheel and the two smaller wheels to rotate at different speeds when maneuvering around corners. Starley also developed a rack-and-pinion steering mechanism for some of his tricycles. Tricycle technology advanced so rapidly that by the early 1880s it was reckoned that the high wheeler was only a mere two miles per hour faster than a good three wheeler. In fact, in an interesting reversal of fortune, penny farthings began to loose their elitist status as youths from the working classes started to acquire second-hand machines. Now tricycles, purchased in ever-growing numbers by the upper classes, became the self-propelled vehicle *de jour*, at least, for another few years.

Starley's high wheeler ruled for no more than a decade, and even though it was little more than a recreational product for young, fit, well-to-do males, it proved to be a stunningly successful bicycle. A highly refined piece of machinery, it was faster than anything on the road and at that time it represented the pinnacle of self-propelled vehicles. There was such a heavy demand for it that bicycle manufacturers showed little interest in developing a more useful device; instead, their efforts were put into advancing the technology of the high wheeler, and before the decade of the 70s had ended such amenities as individually-tensioned tangent-mounted spokes, ball bearings, toe clips, and powerful spoon brakes had been introduced, and the machines grew even lighter and faster. It seemed inconceivable that a low-mount bicycle could compete with a high wheeler in terms of elegance, refinement, speed, and ease of operation, even though the possibility of taking a header at any moment still remained a dangerous reality.

CHAPTER SEVENTEEN

Adam and Eve have adapted to their altered surroundings. They have learned to deal with hills. Adam has become a master at gear shifting. Their daily circumnavigation is carried out in a much slower manner than the brisk 25 miles-per-hour pace they once enjoyed, and although they do not realize it, once again the days have lengthened to compensate. The lion watches them climb his hill every morning, but the rage that act first brought on has mostly disappeared. The cyclists are now thoroughly accustomed to their jerseys, shorts, and sunglasses. They watch each other undress with keen interest, hoping to experience that indescribable sexual rush once again, but that excitement eludes them. Adam and Eve's dreams are no more than unexplained memories. Adam keeps looking at his penis, but it does not oblige him with an erection. Their major problem seems to be the parching thirst that overwhelms them daily, as the increased heat and hills take their toll. Since they can only drink at their noon and evening stops, they decide to ask God for water bottles. This would be a minor request, and they are certain that God would not want them to go thirsty as they ride.

"God, God, Adam and Eve again. We'd like to talk to you," shouts Adam.

Their request is met by a clap of thunder, followed immediately by the materialization of a splendid young man looking very much like Adam. He is, in fact, Adam's spitting image, and like Adam, is dressed in a bicycling jersey, shorts, sunglasses, and shoes. His tanned, muscular body glows with health and tone.

"Hello, Adam. Hello, Eve. Good to see you both," he says in a mellifluous baritone voice.

"Are you God?" asks the confused Eve, looking from one to the other. "You look just like Adam!"

"Eve, how many times are you going to ask that question? Of course I am God. Who else would I be?"

"But you're a man just like Adam. I thought you had to be something different from us," continues the perplexed Eve.

This is confusing to Adam, who had no idea what he looks like. He stares at God-Adam in admiration. "Do I look like that? If I look like that," he thinks, "I'm not bad! Not bad at all!"

"Look," replies the apparition, "I told you, I can be anything or anyone I wish. Do I have to transform myself again just to prove to you that I am God?"

"No," reply the duo in unison.

"We believe you," says Adam, who has no wish to anger the Deity, particularly since he is looking so handsome.

"Well, since you only call on me when you want something, I suppose you have another request," says God-Adam.

Adam makes the pitch. "It's a small one, really. Eden has gotten hilly, the temperature is hotter than it used to be, and the humidity is really bad. We get very thirsty when we ride, and we can't get water until we stop at noon or get back here at night. By then we're parched. We'd like water bottles, so that we can drink as we ride and not be so thirsty all the time."

"Alright. Not a problem. You will have them tomorrow," answers their Maker.

Taken aback by the alacrity with which their request was met, Eve decides to take advantage of God's seeming friendliness.

"Uh, God, I had a dream a while back—at least I think it was a dream—and I'd like to ask you about it."

"Were you riding a solo bike in Iowa?" asks God.

"No, no, it was a dream about my vagina. It made me feel very strange."

"Your vagina, huh?" God does not like where this is going.

"Yes. Something was moving around my vagina, and it went into me. In and out, in and out. It was the strangest feeling. I enjoyed it, but it made me feel funny, too, and it upset me because it left me unsatisfied in some way. My vagina wanted something and I don't know what it was. I woke up and nothing was there."

"Well, who do you suppose gave you that dream?"

"The snake?" Adam blurts out the words in a moment of insight.

"Of course it was the snake! It was not right for him to take advantage of you like that while you were sleeping."

"How did he do that?" wonders Eve.

"He did it with his tail. He is very good with his tail, the slimy reptile!"

"You mean it was his tail going in and out of my vagina? Why would he want to do that?"

"He is trying to get you confused and upset, and it looks like he has succeeded. I am warning you—things are getting dangerous. Do not let him get to you or there could be serious consequences."

Once again, the pair hear God's too-familiar heavy-handed warnings about the snake. He keeps warning them that something bad is going to happen to them if they listen to the snake, but nothing ever does. Now Adam wants to see if God can satisfy his curiosity.

"Uh, God, a while back I was watching Eve take off her clothes and my penis grew and got stiff as a tree trunk. All of a sudden it was hard for me to breathe. Why did it do that? What happened to me?"

Eve chimes in. "And when I saw Adam's penis get hard and long I had the same feeling in my vagina as I did in my dream, when the snake went in and out. Why was that?"

These words do not make God happy.

"Adam, Eve, you are playing with fire. I am warning you again: be careful or you will find yourselves in a lot of trouble. And be careful about asking me for more things."

"But why, God? What did we do?" begins Adam; but with a clap of thunder, God-Adam vanishes.

Once more, God has spoken in riddles. It was the snake who gave Eve her dream so why should *she* have to be careful? And what is it that God is warning them against? Adam and Eve no longer bother to ask themselves what God's words mean. They simply don't know. But Eve is upset at the snake. He had no right to do that to her vagina while she was sleeping.

The pair retire, expecting to see packages containing their water bottles at their feet in the morning. They awake at first light and eagerly search the clearing, but nothing out of the ordinary is to be seen. Disappointed, they perform their morning routines, eat their manna, dress, and are about to mount their tandem when they hear a frantic whirring sound coming from the macadam. They stare in open-mouth wonder as a sweaty bicyclist tears up to them at top speed. At the last second the rider jams on his handbrakes, screeches to a halt, stomps his kickstand down, and leaps off his machine. He is a handsome young fellow, dressed in a T-shirt emblazoned with markings indecipherable to Adam and Eve ("New York Mets"), bicycling shoes and shorts resembling those of our naïve pair, a white helmet, and sunglasses. His hands are covered with fingerless padded gloves. A large brown leather bag is slung over his shoulder, bandoleer style. He reaches into the bag and calls out,

"Delivery for Adam and Eve! That you two?"

The couple respond with dumbfounded nods of their heads.

"Here you go," he says cheerily, and into each pair of uncomprehending hands he thrusts a shrink-wrapped water bottle and cage. He offers Adam a small clipboard with a paper form attached to it and a ball-point pen velcroed to the side. He points:

"Sign here, please."

Adam stands there, water bottle in one hand, clipboard and pen in the other, his mouth still open, unable to respond.

"God?" he questions weakly?

The messenger ignores the query. After a moment he retrieves the clipboard from Adam's unresisting hand, marks an "X" on the form with the pen, and stuffs it all into a pocket in his shoulder bag. He whips a radio out of a holster attached to the strap of his carrier, clicks a button, and calls:

"Double-Oh-Seven at Eden. Mission accomplished. What next?"

The baffled pair hear only a scratchy sound emanate from the black box, unable to make out any words. But the cyclist responds with, "OK God, 10-4."

With that he leaps onto his bicycle, heels up his kick stand and is off, out of the saddle, pedaling hard, his hands down in the drops. In an instant he is moving away at high speed. The pair watch him ride out of sight, finding it difficult to believe what they have seen. Finally, they look at each other, then down at their packages. They cannot explain what has just happened, but they have learned that they cannot explain God. The only thing they are certain of is that God kept his word and delivered the water bottles they hold in their hands.

They tear open the shrink wrap and toss the material into the under-brush, ignoring the fact that they have once again contributed to Eden's burgeoning litter problem. They are holding 20-ounce clear plastic water bottles, each marked with a logo on the bottom reading *Celestial Bicycling Co.* The wide-mouth tops have black screw-on caps with a nipple in the middle. The cages are made of light-weight black anodized aluminum wire attached to curved aluminum plates. Each plate has two holes. Affixed to each cage with a bit of tape is a small ziploc plastic bag containing two allen head machine screws. Adam explains to Eve that the cages attach to the frame tubing, but cannot say exactly how. As if on cue, the snake slithers out of the jungle.

"Hi guys," he greets them happily, "I think you're gonna need some help getting those cages installed."

"Yes, we have to attach the cages to the tandem, but we don't know how to do it," admits Adam.

The boa inspects Adam's cage. "Hmmm. Looks like you need a five millimeter allen wrench."

He shifts his vestigial shoulder and a five millimeter allen wrench, concealed in his tiny armpit, falls to the ground. As he did with the toe clips, he instructs the pair in the use of the tool, and they bolt their cages to the appropriately-spaced and hitherto unnoticed threaded bosses on their tandem. They take their bottles to the stream and as the snake directs them, unscrew the tops and fill them with water. Dropping the filled vessels into their newly-mounted cages the couple note with pride how well-equipped they have become. Adam tells Eve that with these water bottles they are prepared to ride with the best of them in *Ragbray*. But Eve has some business with the boa.

"Snake, I had a dream about my vagina. God said you gave it to me."

"Sure, that was me," replied the reptile, a satisfied grin playing on his thin lips.

"God said you had your tail in my vagina. It was going in and out, in and out. God said it wasn't right for you to do that."

"God said—God said!" mimics the snake. "Always God said. Look—did you like it?"

"Well—yes," admits Eve grudgingly. "It felt good. But why did you do it?"

"What does it matter? I didn't hurt you, did I? And it made you feel good, didn't it?"

"Yes," she admits again, her anger dissipating. "But it also made me want something and I still don't know what it was. And it left me unsatisfied."

"Oh, you'll be satisfied in due time," hisses the snake, his eyes glistening with repressed delight.

Adam breaks in. "Well, a while ago (Adam has no concept of time beyond 'yesterday') I was watching Eve take off her bicycling clothes and my penis got long and stiff. Why did it do that? And I also felt like I wanted something. My whole body wanted something. I was unsatisfied, too."

"Yes," adds Eve, "and when I saw Adam's penis grow long my nipples got hard and I had that same feeling between my legs. It felt like my vagina was dissolving. And I wanted something."

"Don't worry," repeats the wily snake, his tongue flicking with excitement. "You'll both find out what it is you want."

"We asked God about that," adds Adam, "but he only got mad at us and told us we were playing with fire. What did we do?"

"Ah, he's just an old fuddy-duddy," replies the snake. "He's just trying to scare you again.

The pair have more questions for him, but the snake slithers back into the jungle without another word. Once again he leaves them with answers

102

that tell them nothing. What is it they want? When will they get it? What will it be? Is there something wrong with them? Did they do something wrong? What is God warning them against? What is happening to Eden? God talks to them and he makes no sense. The snake talks to them and they have no idea what his words mean. They have dreams and can't explain them. Their daily ride has become hot, hilly, and sweaty. Why has life become so complicated? As they mount their tandem they realize that they have no answers. Only questions.

CHAPTER EIGHTEEN

Bicycle tycoon Albert Pope visits England in 1886. While there he tours the major bicycle factories, all of which are turning out new "Rover"-style low mount safety machines. Pope is amused. He disparages the low mount and announces to the world that the Rover is merely another passing fancy in the topsy-turvy world of self-propelled transportation. He proclaims that the high wheeler was, is, and always will be king of the road. Pope, the father of the modern bicycle, the father of the Good Roads movement, and a pioneer in the soon-to-be automobile business, is dead wrong.

The Rover had been developed only a year before Pope's visit by James Starley's nephew John. Its most obvious features were its cranks and pedals mounted in a hub at the bottom of the down tube, with a chain transferring power to a geared rear wheel; the 36-inch diameter front wheel, smaller than that found on even the most diminutive ordinary; and most importantly, the fact that the saddle was located between the two wheels, providing a secure balance denied to the ordinary. A year later, when the Rover was given two equal-sized 30-inch wheels, the modern safety bicycle was born. The popularity of Rover-style machines swept away high wheelers in England. Nevertheless, elite American riders regarded the safety feature of the low mounts with disdain, noting that the element of danger was what gave cycling its true élan. Still, after viewing the enthusiasm with which imported British safety bikes were accepted, American makers quickly saw the light, and Pope proudly produced his own version of the low-mount chain-driven safety bicycle, the "Columbia," in 1888.

By 1890, with the development of the strong and rigid diamond frame and the invention of the pneumatic tire, the safety bicycle's unforgiving, jittery ride had become a thing of the past and the fate of the high wheeler was incontrovertibly sealed. The inflatable tire, invented in 1888 by John Dunlop, a veterinarian in Belfast, Ireland, who wanted his little son to have a more comfortable ride on his tricycle, soon became standard equipment, and proved to be a major factor in the bicycle boom that consumed Europe, North America, and much of the rest of the world in the early nineties. With this amenity, and with the stiffness supplied by the diamond frame, the safety bicycle swept aside all competition. Racers set blistering records in both long and short distances. Touring cyclists covered the world. Although still an expensive item, prices dipped lower as production increased, still lower as second-hand machines started to become available, and lower yet as Americans acquired bicycles in unprecedented numbers. Eventually, they would even be purchased in hardware and department stores, and repair shops appeared in every town. America went bicycle crazy, as millions of safety machines were purchased in the next few years. It seemed that the bicycle had finally fulfilled its promise as a self-propelled vehicle for the working classes.

No longer faced with the prospect of taking a header every time they mounted their wheels, women deserted their tricycles and took to the safety bicycle in dizzying numbers. The trend was first set in motion by those of high social standing, but they were quickly joined by middle and lower class women. To the horror of many men, fully a third of all new sales were made to the fair sex. Appropriate bicycle garb was a problem at first, but binding street garments gave way to looser clothing and then to "bloomers," or baggy knicker-like pants, worn with stockings. The cycling industry cooperated by producing a lady's model, with a dropped frame for easier mounting and dismounting. Following the law of unintended consequences, the bicycle not only provided transportation for women of all classes, it liberated them. For the first time, the distaff half of the population had the ability to go where it wanted, when it wanted, and under its own power. This change did not take place without notice. Young men on bicycles had the same ability, and there was concern that representatives of the two sexes might decide to go to the same place at the same time. There was also a genuine if misplaced fear that young women could suffer a variety of ills from cycling, ranging from the loss of child-bearing ability to sexual arousal from the friction of the saddle.

The popularity of the bicycle had other social consequences. Since it was no longer merely a plaything of the elite, exclusive bicycle clubs gave way to more democratic organizations, where men and women of all social classes were united by their love of cycling. Formerly, a workman on foot was literally required to look up to a gentleman or a person of title seated in a carriage or on a horse. Now both were mounted on steeds of iron and rubber. Now they passed each other moving under their own power, at the same speed, and neither man was elevated. Boss and worker alike took to their wheels on weekends, leaving the busy city behind and heading for the country for fresh air and adventure. No matter what their social standing, they traveled the same roads, strained up the same hills, got wet together when it rained, and slaked their thirst and hunger at the same country taverns. It was not without reason that the bicycle was called "the great leveler." It was even heralded as a boon to the environment, since it displaced smelly, waste-producing horses and noisy carriages on city streets.

For most of the 1890s bicycle manufacturing was the dominant industry in the United States, and its specialized tools and mass production techniques were the envy of the rest of the world. Once again Albert Pope was in the lead, pumping out units at the rate of one per minute in a vast factory complex that created its own nickel-steel hollow tubing for frames, rubber for tires and inner tubes, and components such as spokes, brakes, ball bearings, hubs, chains, gears, and pedals. This was mass production on a scale exceeded only a few years later by Henry Ford's automobile works.

Nevertheless, it all came to a halt in 1897. The boom was over. The reasons were many, including the saturation of the market, the emergence of the motorcycle and automobile, and the loss of the cachet of exclusiveness. Primarily, though, the bicycle lost favor because its astonishing popularity was—once again—mainly a fad, destined to end sooner or later. To the socially elite, the motor car was now the personal transporter de jour. Despite this, bicycles continued to be made, bought, and ridden, but as commuting tools and utility vehicles, not as social or fashion statements, or merely as machines for healthy exercise. The boom ended in Europe as well, although there the bicycle's recreational aspect had taken hold much more solidly than in the United States.

Out of the ashes of the collapse of the bicycle's manufacturing base grew the automobile. Former manufacturers like Pope, or mechanics like Henry Ford, became auto makers. The scores of bicycle repair shops that dotted the nation metamorphosed into automobile service stations. Many of the mechanical principles that helped develop the bicycle, such as chain drives, ball bearings, differential gears, rack-and-pinion steering, spoked wheels, and pneumatic tires, were incorporated into the motor car. The burgeoning aviation industry also owed much to the bicycle, with Orville and Wilbur Wright, two cycle mechanics from Dayton, Ohio developing a flying machine solidly based on bicycle technology.

The bicycle would never regain the ownership of the roads it enjoyed in the gay nineties, and never again would bicycling be experienced as it was then. Although it was not until the very end of the century that American makers would develop the freewheel, and a three-speed hub that allowed a modicum of control over gearing, the machines were nevertheless light, efficient, and fairly comfortable. Utilizing the good macadamized roads available in and around larger cities, bicycles did not yet need to share them with automobiles, trucks, motorcycles, or any other motorized vehicles. The camaraderie of the bicycle broke down the rigid class system inherited from Europe, and it never recovered. Women found that they had the strength and the character to ride with men, and that they benefited from the exercise. Bicycling brought about a revolution in feminine clothing, and it emancipated women in other ways as well. It was the bicycle that set the stage for personal transportation in the twentieth century. And it was the tandem bicycle that in 1892 inspired the English tunesmith Harry Dacre to write:

Daisy, Daisy,
Give me your answer, do.
I'm half crazy,
All for the love of you.
It won't be a stylish marriage,
I can't afford a carriage.
But you'll look sweet,
Upon the seat,
Of a bicycle built for two.

CHAPTER NINETEEN

Adam and Eve have become adept at holding a handlebar with one hand and drinking from a water bottle with the other. Adam's expert shifting skills continue to impress Eve. The increased demands of their circumnavigations have improved their already splendid physical conditioning, and their bodies glow with health and tone. But Adam and Eve are unhappy. Their strenuous six-day-a-week cycling regimen has become wearying. Faced with hills, increases in temperature and humidity, and longer days in the saddle, they begin to look on their daily ride as work and their ration of manna cakes as payment, and they are not satisfied with their wages. Finally, one morning at breakfast, Adam put their concerns into words.

"We have to work so hard to make our daily ride around Eden and all we get for it is this manna crap. I'm getting tired of manna."

Adam begins a familiar mantra: "You should eat some pancakes, Eve. You wouldn't believe how wonderful they taste, the way they smell, and the way they warm your stomach when they go down."

But now he adds another thought: "I think we should ask God for pancakes."

Eve has never tasted pancakes, but she has an idea. Maybe the pancakes would satisfy that unknown physical yearning they'd both experienced. She shares the concept with Adam, who agrees with alacrity.

"Sure, that must be it! You're smart, Eve! I tell you, I was never so happy as when I ate those pancakes. Pancakes must be what we both need to make us feel satisfied."

"OK," says Eve, "but will we ask for pancakes three times a day? God might think we were greedy if we did that."

"You're right. Besides, I don't think I could ride in the afternoon if we had pancakes for the midday meal. In my dream they made me fall asleep."

"Well, we don't want that to happen. And we wouldn't want it to happen in the morning, either, or we wouldn't be able to ride at all."

The couple agree. They'll ask God to substitute pancakes for manna at the evening meal, and once again, they call on the Deity. This time there are no flames, no heavy footsteps, no claps of thunder. Instead, a man of Adam's height appears on the macadam and walks into their clearing. He appears to be in his early 50s, neatly dressed in a pin-striped double-breasted blue suit, a white cotton shirt, a solid blue silk tie, and dark brown wing-tip shoes. His greying hair is neatly combed. With his square jaw, jowly cheeks, five-o'clock shadow, and ski-jump nose, he resembles Richard Nixon. He approaches Adam and Eve, neither of whom has any intention of asking him to verify his identity.

"Good morning, Adam; good morning, Eve. It's a beautiful day, isn't it?" God-Nixon sniffs the air appreciatively, hunches his shoulders, raises his arms, and flexes his biceps. "What can I do for you this morning?"

Emboldened by God's good humor, Adam gets right to the point. He has a carefully prepared speech.

"God, it's getting harder and harder for us to ride our tandem around Eden. All we get for it is manna, manna, manna, three times a day. It's not that we don't appreciate it, but manna is pretty tasteless. We think we deserve something better for the work we do. For our evening meal we'd like to have hot pancakes instead of manna."

Eve chimes in. "And we think the pancakes are what we've been wanting. The last time we talked I told you about the dream with my vagina, and how I awoke feeling unsatisfied."

"And I had that same unsatisfied feeling, the time I saw Eve undress and my penis got long and stiff," adds Adam. "Remember? I told you about that, too."

Eve continues. "We think the pancakes will make us feel satisfied. We think that's what we've been wanting."

God is torn. Adam and Eve want to substitute food for sex, which is just fine with him. A daily supply of hot pancakes will take some work, but still, God decides, it will be worth it.

"Alright. When you return from your ride tonight you shall have hot pancakes. But this one is not going to be easy, and you would really do well to stop asking me for things."

110

"Thank you, God," they chorus. God-Nixon turns on his heel and strides off down the macadam path.

Our cyclists can barely contain their excitement. Tonight they will eat pancakes.

"Delicious, hot, golden-brown pancakes," croons Adam.

He has described these pancakes, their appearance, their texture, their shape, their color, their temperature, and their effect on him so often, and in such detail, that Eve is beside herself with anticipation. "Tonight we will get hot pancakes," she repeats to herself, over and over. Naturally, all that anticipation only makes the day go slower. The noon manna tastes even blander than usual. The sun is low in the west when the weary pair return to their encampment. They expect to find the pancakes in the place they always find their manna; instead, the middle of the clearing is occupied by a griddle of the type Adam saw in his dream. On the griddle are six large, beautiful, steaming, golden-brown pancakes, done to a turn. To the left of the griddle is a table, behind which is sitting a man, the very image of the volunteer who collected the money in Adam's dream.

Eve asks Adam, *sotto voce*: "Is he God?"

"I don't think so," replies Adam in a whisper. "He looks like one of the pancake men from my dream."

Seeing the couple arrive the volunteer gets up, spatulas the cakes into two paper plates, wordlessly presents one to each cyclist, and returns to his seat behind the table. Adam shows Eve how to tear off a piece of the cake and convey it to her mouth, but Eve has little need for a lesson. They consume the cakes greedily, both moaning with pleasure, reveling in the taste, smell, texture and warmth of the food. Their lips glisten as the juices run down their chins. Their heads nod back and forth appreciatively, and their eyes tear with joy. Their hands chop the air in gestures of delight. They sink to their knees from sheer bliss. Eve is overcome by the taste of the unfamiliar food. Why have they never realized how hungry they became after cycling all day? This is what they needed, they tell themselves. This is what they needed to satisfy themselves. Satisfaction is pancakes. Pancakes is everything Adam said and more.

Their meal completed, the pair toss their paper plates into the under-brush and refresh themselves in the stream. They end the day sitting on the grass, watching the sun set and savoring each other's companionship. Eve rests her head on Adam's shoulder, and he puts his arm around her and draws her closer. They remain in that intimate position until the stars appear. Finally, they lie down next to each other, their hands touching, and immediately fall into a contented slumber. The boa slithers out of the jungle, looks at the sleeping innocents, throws his head back, and emits a strangled sound of mirth.

Every evening Adam and Eve return from their ride to find pancakes on the griddle. As soon as they arrive the volunteer gets up from his chair, serves them, and sits back down. By the time they finish their meal he and the griddle have vanished. The pancakes give them great satisfaction, and after their evening bath they sit with their arms around each other, watching the setting sun. Pancakes is happiness. Their companionship is happiness. Arms around each other is happiness. Adam and Eve are happy.

But conditions in Eden are about to change again, and not for the bet-ter. Passing the lion's area the next morning they are struck by the unmistakable stench of fresh blood. Adam suggests the unthinkable: to stop the tandem and investigate. Only a few steps off the macadam they discover the lion devouring a freshly killed gazelle. With his paws planted firmly on the lifeless carcass, his face is buried deep within the laid-open body of his prey. He is consuming the dead creature's heart, ripping it from the corpse with his sharp incisors. He looks up angrily as Adam and Eve approach, a fierce and menacing look on his blood-rimmed face, and emits an intimidating roar of warning. The horrified pair retreat imme-diately, remount, and hurriedly pedal out of the area. They are shaken at what they have seen.

"That was blood," shudders Eve, "the lion was eating the gazelle's blood."

"Maybe the lion somehow made the gazelle cease to exist," wonders Adam, the concept of death totally foreign to him.

"But why would the lion want to do that to the gazelle? If he's hungry, why doesn't he just eat his lion manna?"

Adam has no answer, and the rest of the day's ride is spent in silence, the couple brooding over the unexpected and ominous vision of predation. They search for an explanation, but there is none. "What is happening to Eden?" they wonder. Even their evening pancakes, served up by the silent volunteer, fails to alter their dark mood. They have just finished their meal when the snake sashays into the clearing. Unlike the couple, he is in high spirits.

"Hey, kids, got yourselves some nice pancakes now, huh?"

"God was really good about it," responds Eve. "We told him we thought that the pancakes would give us the satisfaction we never got when you put your tail in my vagina, and when Adam's penis got long and hard."

"Well," snickers the snake, barely able to contain himself, "do the pancakes work? Are you satisfied?"

"Oh yes," agrees Adam. "We really feel satisfied now."

The snake bursts out in laughter, cackling as only a boa constrictor can cackle, tears streaming from his eyes, his forked tongue wagging back and forth, his tiny vestigial arms trying to hold his bursting sides, his long body writhing in mirth, his tail vibrating like a rattle. Adam and Eve have never heard the boa make those sounds, but they seem benign, and soon they, too, are laughing. It feels good, and it gives a needed lift to their dark frame of mind. Finally, the snake gets hold of himself.

"So pancakes is what you needed to relieve those feelings, huh?" he asks.

The pair's eager "Oh, yes!" sends him into another sustained outburst of laughter, in which Adam and Eve again join, if for no other reason than laughing is nice. Finally the boa is too weak to laugh anymore. This Adam, this Eve—God's creatures—they are really something else! Talk about naïve! This is rich!

But Adam has other things on his mind. "Snake, we saw something terrible today. The lion was eating the insides of a gazelle, eating its blood.

It looked awful. What happened to the gazelle?"

"The lion killed it."

"What do you mean, 'killed it'?"

"He made it so that it was no longer alive. Do you remember the first time you spoke to God? Do you remember how bad that was?"

"Oh, yes," breathes Eve.

"Well, if God had wanted to, he could have made you dead on the spot. He could have killed you, right there."

"Do you mean he could have made us not exist?"

"Oh no, you'd still exist alright—but you'd be dead." Your heart would stop beating. You would stop breathing. Your blood would stop going around in your body. You would no longer have any consciousness. Your flesh would rot. You would no longer be Adam or Eve. You'd be nothing but dead meat, like the gazelle."

Adam tries to process this information.

"How did the lion kill it?"

"He followed the gazelle and when it wasn't looking he jumped on it, got hold of its neck with his teeth and broke it. That killed it."

"That must have really hurt the gazelle."

"Yeah, but not for long. The lion killed it pretty quickly."

"But why was he eating the gazelle?"

"He was hungry."

"But doesn't God give him manna, like he gives us?"

"Yes, but he was tired of his lion manna. He wanted something that tasted better."

"Couldn't he have eaten pancakes?" queries Eve?

"No, pancakes is not his food. He likes to kill his food and eat it."

Adam and Eve only dimly understand this repugnant news, but it is upsetting. Their thoughts are whirling. Death is a concept foreign to them. In fact, up to now, death has been a concept foreign to the Garden as well. They realize that death was a very bad thing for the gazelle. They wonder why the lion killed it; but they cannot connect the dots. One would think they might see a correlation between themselves and the lion both tiring of their God-given sustenance, but it never occurs to them. And had they been even a little more perceptive, they might have realized that the gazelle's death meant that the lion was on the hunt, and that this signaled a basic change in the way that Eden operated. But Adam and Eve have not been programmed with that much insight.

"Oh, cheer up, kids," chides the sly snake as he glides back into the jungle. "It's not like one little gazelle makes any difference. And it makes the lion happy, so what's the harm?"

The couple accept the snake's easy explanation and prepare for their dip in the stream. Alone now, they remove their bicycling clothing. Adam sees Eve's nude body silhouetted against the setting sun, accentuating the lithesome curves of her shapely legs, her toned abdomen, her firm breasts, and her rounded buttocks. In an instant he becomes aroused, his penis hard and stiff, his testicles ascending into his scrotum, his body flushed and warm.

"Eve—Eve." he calls in a strangled voice.

"Adam—your penis—it's long and hard again!" she answers

"And your nipples are sticking out and your body is turning red."

"And my vagina feels all wet and slippery, too, but I can't help it. You look so handsome and trim, and your muscles are bulging. With your penis long and stiff and sticking straight out like that I have this intense desire. I want something! What is it?"

"I don't know," croaks Adam. "All I know is my penis feels like it's about to burst."

"My vagina feels like it's about to melt."

"I have that feeling again—I want something and I don't know what it is. I'm going crazy!"

"I have that same feeling, and I can hardly stand it. We thought pancakes was what we wanted. We must have been wrong."

"I guess so. What is it we want?"

"I don't know! I hope we find out soon."

Adam and Eve stare at each other for a while, breathing heavily, frustration etched on their faces. They are without the slightest understanding of the physiological changes gripping their young, vital bodies, but whatever it is they want is not to be revealed tonight. Tonight they splash around in the cold water of the stream until their emotions subside. Tonight they are too disturbed to sit next to each other and watch the sun set. Tonight they can think of nothing to do but pace up and down like caged animals; but as darkness comes they lie down and finally fall into their usual dreamless sleep. In the middle of the night the snake crawls into the clearing, dragging something in his mouth. He drops it near the pair and disappears back into the jungle. It is a publication of some sort. The cover reads *Celestial Bicycling Co. 2007 Catalog.*

CHAPTER TWENTY

The kind of machine I ride—the modern "safety" bicycle, with its chain drive, diamond frame, and pneumatic tires—arrived on the scene just before the dawn of the twentieth century. It was a big improvement over the old high wheelers, and it didn't take the military long to figure out that with its speed, maneuverability, reliability, and ability to carry heavy loads, it could serve in the army. It had many advantages over a horse. It was faster, it didn't leave waste products behind for trackers to spot, and it didn't require food, water, rest, grooming, or any upkeep other than an occasional oiling of the chain and the bearings. A good rider could easily do up to 100 miles a day, and keep it up day after day, while transporting up to 100 pounds of food, water, baggage, weapons, and ammunition. The diamond frame itself was so strong that it could support two tons or more before deforming. The bicycle was at a disadvantage where roads were bad or non-existent, but under those circumstances the horse didn't do that well either. And with a bike you could just get off and push it—or carry it, if need be.

This fellow Albert Pope, the guy who made more bicycles than anyone else at that time, promoted the new safety bicycle to the U. S. army. He even gave 40 brand new machines to the Connecticut National Guard. Of course, he hoped for a large order of bikes from the military, but they showed little interest. That was sort of short-sighted, since it was obvious to the armies of some other countries that a soldier on a bicycle makes an ideal messenger—remember, this is before the radio or the telephone. Bicycle-mounted couriers and scouts were successfully used during the Boer War, and in country after country military cycle couriers, sometimes alone, sometimes in relays, set record times delivering dispatches.

Before long some overly-ambitious military guys thought that the bike could not only be used for carrying messages, but could also be used in the cavalry, artillery, and infantry. They thought that cycle-mounted cavalry was a logical extension of the bicycle's role in replacing the horse. After all, they reasoned, a bicycle presented a far smaller target than a horse and so was less likely to be hit by enemy fire; and even if it was put out of action, one could be reassembled from spare parts. Also, bicycles were silent, raised little or no dust, and didn't leave tracks that revealed the direction of travel. That all sounded good, but when reality set in it was realized that a trooper on a benign thirty-pound machine was required to devote almost all his attention to locomotion and steering. He could hardly replace the combination of a saber-waving warrior mounted on a fierce-looking half-ton beast, inspiring shock and awe as they charged down on an enemy. Not only that, waving a saber or firing a rifle while riding a bicycle was next to impossible. The concept of bicycle cavalry had a short life.

Because the bicycle has this remarkable ability to carry hundreds of times its own weight, it seemed reasonable to mount machine guns, cannon, and other heavy weapons on bicycles and tricycles, or at least, drag them behind. But the problem is getting all that mass into motion. It's really difficult for a poor soldier on a solo bike to haul large, bulky, heavy weaponry over any distance, and impractical to expect that the ordnance could be fired while moving. They tried all sorts of things to overcome this: they used tricycles, tandem tricycles, and even rows of solo bikes, tandems, and tricycles, all hooked together by poles, and all pulling together to move the heavy load. Most of these rigs were able to propel themselves and their loads on level ground, but they almost all failed when they had to haul their burdens up hills. Still, if the bike wasn't suited for carrying artillery, it could be an effective replacement for the pack mule. During the Vietnam War thousands of Viet Cong delivered supplies to their troops by pushing bicycles down the Ho Chi Minh trail, each machine loaded with as much as 450 pounds of matériel. The American High Command couldn't believe that this was happening. How could a bicycle, a device that in their eyes was nothing more than a child's toy, possibly be used as an effective mode of supply?

The bicycle did claim a place in the infantry, though. Since the days of the Roman conquerors a column could march about 20 miles per day; but an infantryman with full gear, mounted on a bike, could maintain a ten-mile per hour pace and keep it up for eight to ten hours a day. In unfavorable weather or bad terrain he simply dismounted and pushed or carried his machine. Not only would the bicycle bring him to the field of battle far more quickly, he'd be comparatively fresh and more able to engage the enemy. Also, it meant not having to deal with horses, although it didn't take the bigwigs long to figure out that the supporting mechanism of the troops—the wagons, kitchens, supplies, surgeries, artillery, and so forth—were all horse-drawn and would be left far behind; so the supposed advantage of the cycle-mounted trooper was less useful than might be imagined at first sight. Still, to prove the point, in 1897 a corps of 20 African-American soldiers rode 2,000 miles, from Missoula, Montana to St. Louis, Missouri. It was a tough trip, through all sorts of weather and difficult terrain, but they averaged a very respectable 50 miles a day. Their heavy-duty machines weighed in at 32 pounds, and to that was added the weight of the rider plus cooking equipment, food, water, coat, blanket, tent, arms, and ammunition. And except for one, they all made it. Those guys were one tough bunch!

Imagine columns of bicycle-mounted soldiers sweeping rapidly across vast distances, dropping their machines, and successfully engaging an unsuspecting enemy. This scenario actually happened in every major war of the twentieth century. One of the most significant uses of bicycle infantry occurred in 1937, when the Japanese employed 50,000 bicycle-mounted troops in their invasion of China. Japanese forces used bicycles to spectacularly good effect again, in 1941, minutes before their attack on Pearl Harbor, when they invaded Malaya and captured Singapore. The British never knew what hit them, and it was probably the supreme example of the usefulness of cycle-mounted infantry in the history of modern warfare.

Given that infantry frequently need to be transported by rail or ship, and often have to operate in areas with poor or non-existent roads and sometimes cross bodies of water, you'd think that a folding bicycle might play an important role in warfare. British and German paratroopers used them in World War II, but after that the military folding bicycle was pretty much ignored until the end of the twentieth century, when the U.S. Marine Corps developed a modern foldable mountain bike, once again primarily for the use of paratroopers.

These days bicycles continue to have military uses, ranging from ferrying airmen up and down long flight lines on airfields, to laying telegraph and telephone wires, to patrolling perimeters in battlefield situations. But for the most part the bicycle's participation in modern warfare is still limited to the function at which it clearly excels: carrying a message.

CHAPTER TWENTY ONE

Eve awakes to find Adam staring wonderingly at the *Celestial Bicycling Co.* catalog.

"Look Eve," he tells her, "I don't know what this is or how it got here, but it's full of images of all this bicycle stuff."

Eve looks at the catalog with wonder. Neither of them suspected that anything like this could exist. Could it have come from God? Over their morning manna the couple leaf through the thin pages, staring at the pictures, their features mirroring their amazement. They have never seen photographs before, but they can readily identify the colorful images of their toe clips, shoes, jerseys, shorts, helmets, sunglasses, and water bottles, and they assume that everything they see in the slim volume represents real items, even the species members wearing and using the equipment. Jerseys and shorts are near the beginning. Shoes come soon after that. Sunglasses are there, too. Helmets are in the middle, followed by toe clips and water bottles. The rest of the catalog consists of bicycle components such wheels, spokes, tires, saddles, pedals, handlebars, and drive train apparatus. They see accoutrements they never dreamed of: socks, jackets, rain gear, energy bars, sports drinks, rear racks, panniers, handlebar bags, transporters, cyclometers, heart monitors, work stands, tire pumps, and specialized tools, all of which are meaningless to them.

The last section is devoted to pictures of solo bicycles.

Adam remembers the bike he rode in his dream. How fleet it was, how light and nimble it felt, how easily it steered, how smooth the gearing was, how neatly the indexed shifting worked, how effortlessly it braked. Eve is fascinated by the representations of the sort of machine that Adam has so often described to her. She develops an instant desire to own and ride one, to get off the rear saddle of the tandem where her view is obstructed by Adam's back, to gain the freedom of proceeding under her own pedal power, to do her own shifting and braking, to mount and dismount by herself. The catalog's pages are filled with all sorts of bicycles—mountain bikes, all-terrain bikes, comfort bikes, cyclocross bikes, touring bikes—but Adam only shows Eve the road bicycle, the wheel he rode in his dream, the machine with a triple chain ring, an eight-speed rear cluster, and indexed shifters in the brake levers.

"You know, Eve," reasons Adam, "we thought pancakes was what we wanted, that they would satisfy that strange desire we have. But it didn't work. It wasn't pancakes. You know what I think? I think what we really need to satisfy us is solo bikes. We could go much faster with solo bikes. (Adam is mistaken on this point. The two wheels of a tandem have less rolling resistance than the four wheels of two solo machines, and since the captain breaks the wind for the stoker, the tandem generates less wind resistance than two solo bikes. But try telling that to Adam.) We could each shift our own gears, too—I'll teach you how; and it's a lot easier to get off and on a solo bike. And with all the hills we have in Eden now, we could really use the granny gear on this bike."

Eve is impressed by this long speech, particularly since it meshes exactly with her own desires. Eve is about to give voice to the thought they both hold—to ask God for solo bikes—when the snake glides out of the jungle. He is barely able to restrain his excitement.

"Hey kids, what do you have there?" he hisses.

"We found this when we woke up this morning," says Adam, waving the catalog. "How do you suppose it got here?"

"Ah, the latest *Celestial Bicycling* catalog!" the boa exclaims happily. "Now how do *you* suppose it got here?" he counters, shaking with mirth.

But Adam has already forgotten his question. He is far more interested in the contents of the booklet he holds.

"What is a 'catalog'?" he asks.

"It's a list of things," replies the boa. "That's what you have there—a listing of all the parts and accessories for bicycles, with pictures. Find anything interesting?"

"Yes," chimes in Eve. She shows the snake the picture of the solo road bike.

"Ah," says the reptile. "Road bike. Aluminum frame. Carbon-fiber fork. Triple chain ring, eight-speed rear cluster. Indexed shifters mounted in the brake levers. A neat machine."

"Do you think God would give us each one of these?" asks Eve.

"I don't see why not. He wants you to be happy, doesn't he?"

"Well yes, he seems to, and we think solo bikes are what we really need. For a while we thought the pancakes would satisfy our strange desires, but we were wrong. We both got them again, last night, real bad, right after we ate."

"The snake cannot believe his ears. This is the fruit of God's imagination? This is what he creates in his own image? These *schmucks*? These *Chaim Yonkels*? They think *bicycles* are what they need? He struggles to contain his glee.

"Yeah, yeah, go ahead, check in with God," he says, as he glides back into the jungle, his body shuddering with repressed laughter. "He'll give you what you want."

But this is not the time to talk with God. This is the time to mount the tandem and begin the day's ride. Conversation soon ensues.

"Do *you* think we should ask God for solo bikes?" asks Eve.

Adam is more than willing, but he hesitates, nevertheless. He realizes that this request will dwarf all the others. A bicycle is a lot bigger than a helmet or a water bottle.

"Maybe we should, but solo bikes—that's a *big* thing to ask for. It's not a small thing like a water bottle. God keeps telling us that it's not a good idea to ask for anything else. He says that every time he gives us something. He keeps warning us that something is going to happen, even though nothing ever does." (Adam and Eve have not yet made a connection between their growing materialism and the deteriorating conditions in Eden.) "But if he really gets mad there's no telling what he'll do."

"Yes," agrees Eve, "He keeps saying that we shouldn't ask for anything else, but in fact, he gets more and more agreeable every time we talk to him. He's been so nice lately, and seems happy to give us anything we want. I think we should ask him."

Adam is easily convinced. "I guess you're right. He *was* in a good mood the last time we talked to him. He not only gave us the pancakes, he gave us the species member from *Ragbray* to serve them to us every night when we get home. That was nice."

"Let's ask him tonight," urges Eve, "after we have our pancakes."

Adam readily acquiesces. Giving up their tandem for solo bikes is a big move, and the couple spend the rest of the day in happy anticipation.

That night, the pancakes eaten and still warm in their stomachs, paper plates tossed into the underbrush, the couple call on their Maker once again.

"God, we'd like to talk to you," calls Adam.

A few moments later a small, stooped, skinny, narrow-shouldered, elderly man shambles into the clearing. His mobile, wide-eyed face is framed with thick, black-rimmed spectacles. His sparse hair is uncombed and a day's growth of beard is visible on his weather-beaten face. His lower lip droops and his jaw is slack. He is wearing an open-neck shirt, a well-worn, loose-fitting pullover sweater, shapeless corduroy pants, and brown loafers. He is the spitting image of an 85-year old Woody Allen.

"Hi Adam, Hi Eve." He greats them mildly, a dreamy smile on his lips.

"How are you this evening, God?" ventures Adam.

"Oh, I'm fine, Adam," replies God-Allen, with no trace of the impatient anger he expressed the last time Adam tried to make small talk. "Just a few aches and pains. A little indigestion once in a while. Maybe a little constipation. Nothing serious. You shouldn't worry."

Adam gets right to the point. "We have another request, God, and we hope you won't be upset by it."

"Nah, nah, how bad could it be!"

Eve decides to set the scene. "Remember when we asked for pancakes? We love them! They taste delicious after a hard day's ride around Eden. And we really appreciate the species member who serves them to us every night. But the pancakes didn't satisfy that strange desire we both have. Just last night it happened again. Adam's penis grew long and stiff, my nipples got hard, and my vagina got all slippery. We both got warm all over. Then we both wanted it, whatever it is, and we didn't calm down until after we'd both jumped into the stream."

"Ah, jumping into the stream, cooling off a bit, that's good," responds God-Allen with an approving nod.

Adam joins in, holding up his copy of the *Celestial Bicycling Co. 2007* catalog. "Well, the thing is, we found this—this catalog with pictures when we woke up this morning. We think (God knows what is coming and he is not pleased) what we want is solo bikes. That's what we've been needing all this time (God does not like this). The tandem only has 10 gears. It doesn't have indexed shifting, and the shift levers are on the down tube (God is really getting angry). And Eden has gotten so hilly we really need granny gears. We'd like solo bikes with 24 gears, indexed shifting, and shifters in the brakes levers. We don't want to ride the tandem any more."

God is mad. God is furious. These ungrateful creatures! These ingrates! These little shit heads! These cockers! These *verkakte Kinder!* So what if the snake (who else?) gave them that catalog? What if they *are* proposing to substitute exercise for sex? How could they turn their backs on their God-given transportation? JUST WHO DO THEY THINK THEY ARE, ASKING FOR SOLO BICYCLES WITH 24 FANCY SPEEDS AND GRANNY GEARS AND LA-DI-DA INDEXED SHIFTING? I'LL GIVE THEM GRANNY GEARS AND INDEXED SHIFTING ALRIGHT!

With an ear-splitting crash of thunder Woody Allen is gone, replaced by the eight-foot giant they'd seen previously, when they'd asked for bicycling clothes and sunglasses. As last time, God is wearing a flowing white robe and sandals and holding a staff. But this time he is standing in the center of a circle of flame, and he is spitting mad. He shifts his staff to his other hand and extends one long arm. His forefinger, crackling with a bluish energy discharge, points directly at them. His irate eyes bore through the astonished pair, and his voice fills them with terror as they sink to their knees. His words are dreadful.

"YOU INGRATES! YOU TWO ARE UNBELIEVABLE. NO MATTER HOW MANY TIMES I TELL YOU IT IS NOT A GOOD IDEA TO ASK FOR ANYTHING ELSE YOU COME BACK TO ME WITH MORE REQUESTS. WELL NOW YOU HAVE DONE IT! YOU HAVE

PUSHED ME OVER THE EDGE. SOLO BICYCLES, 24 GEARS, SHIFTERS IN THE BRAKE LEVERS, GRANNY GEARS! THE TANDEM I GAVE YOU IS NOT GOOD ENOUGH FOR YOU ANY MORE, IS THAT IT? TEN SPEEDS ARE NOT ENOUGH? FRICTION SHIFTING NO LONGER WORKS FOR YOU? DOWN TUBE SHIFTERS DO NOT CUT IT ANYMORE?"

Adam and Eve are stunned at the sudden change in God's manifestation, his frightening mien, his threatening posture, his pointing forefinger, the circle of fire, the thunderous words and their horrible import. They draw back and clutch each other's arms. Each thinks, "Uh-oh, we're in for it now. God is really going to punish us. He's going to make us not exist."

Adam thinks fast. "God, God," he pleads. "We didn't mean it! We're happy riding the tandem. It's a great bike, God! It's the best! It's really all we need! We don't really want those granny gears—we can make it up the hills on the tandem just fine! Please don't make us not exist!"

But God is not to be placated. "YOU TURNED YOUR BACKS ON YOUR GOD-GIVEN TRANSPORTATION. WELL I AM FED UP WITH BOTH OF YOU! YOU SAY YOU LIKE THE TANDEM? ALRIGHT! IT IS BACK TO THE TANDEM AND BACK TO SQUARE ONE FOR YOU, BOTH OF YOU!"

And with thunder and lightning crashing around the clearing, God vanishes, leaving Adam and Eve stunned and dazed as the circle of fire burns itself to ashes.

CHAPTER TWENTY TWO

The lion stirs, awakened by the day. He hears something—a distant rhythmic whirring—more a sensation than a sound. His sharp eyes search the landscape, his attention drawn to the now insistent thrumming. The hum grows more audible, and his abdomen feels the ground vibrate with its approach. He begins to make out the source of the disturbance, approaching rapidly from his right, on a smooth, five-foot-wide ribbon of macadam that curves through the Garden. The object sweeps by him: a tandem bicycle, propelled by two figures. The lion watches as it swiftly disappears on his left. His curiosity has been satisfied. He is no longer interested. Right now a nap is more important.

Although they have been cycling since shortly after first light, the occupants of the tandem do not stop to rest. Neither cyclist appears to be working hard, nor are they perspiring, although they are traveling at a speed of 25 miles an hour. The macadam they ride on slopes at a two percent downgrade. The ambient temperature is a pleasant 72 degrees Fahrenheit, and the relative humidity is 40 percent. With a 10-mile-per-hour wind at their backs, with their legs spinning like well-oiled pistons in a pedaling cadence of 80 revolutions per minute, with their chain fixed in a 100 gear, with the wheels of their self-propelled vehicle thrumming monotonously on the road, Adam and Eve are circumnavigating Eden on their red chromium-molybdenum ten-speed Schwinn tandem.

Adam's attention is fixed unswervedly on the road ahead. His task is to keep his machine centered on the macadam and to maintain a speed of 25 miles per hour. With the smooth, downward-sloping roadbed, the unvarying cadence, the 100 gear, and the wind at their backs, the pace is not difficult to sustain and the couple's tempo is unvarying. This is what they have been made to do. Unlike Adam, Eve is not distracted by the need to keep the tandem centered on the macadam; nevertheless, the kaleidoscopic view of the flora and fauna that line the path do not demand her attention. Instead, her gaze is fixed on Adam's muscular back, his well-formed trapeziums, rhomboids, and deltoids, as he hunches over the drops of his handlebars.

At noon the couple dismount, lean their bicycle against a tree, and walk a few steps to a nearby sylvan glade. They are completely and unselfconsciously naked. They seat themselves on the ground. Manna appears before them, in the form of four small, soft, round, white cakes, each supplying one-sixth of their daily nutritional requirements. They consume two cakes each, conveying the bland, flaky substance to their mouths with their fingers. A nearby stream provides cool, refreshing water. They rest, ignoring each other's presence. They do not share any activity other than riding the tandem. Except for turning their pedals in a forced unison, they do not communicate with each other in any way. Wordlessly, they return to the tandem and continue their ride. When the sun is low on the western horizon the cyclists halt again, now returned to the point from which they had started early that morning. Once again they find cakes of manna and a stream of water close to hand. Adam and Eve have been bicycling all day and have covered 200 miles. As darkness falls they stretch out on the soft grass and immediately fall into dreamless sleep. They sleep together, but apart. They eliminate bodily wastes with as much concern for privacy as the lion.

The next day in the Garden of Eden passes much the same as the first. The lion rises with the rosy-fingered dawn, eats his morning meal, and settles down to see if the tandem will pass again. What else does he have to do? He does not have to hunt; sustenance is provided for him, as it is for all the denizens of this wondrous Garden. His sharp claws and huge incisors are capable of ripping prey to shreds, but there is no prey. He does not even know what prey is. In fact, none of the animals need to hunt or seek food. Insects need not eat plant life; birds need not eat berries and fruit; no living creature, no flora or fauna, has a natural enemy. All is provided for them in this delightful environment, this splendid Garden. So the lion waits, and is soon rewarded: Adam and Eve pass by on their tandem at 25 miles per hour, pedaling at a cadence of 80 revolutions per minute in their 100 gear. As it was yesterday, and as it will be tomorrow, Adam's attention is focused on the macadam. Eve's attention is focused on Adam's back. So goeth the days in Eden. Life is easy; life is good; life is goddamn boring.

Because.

God has pressed the "undo" key on the celestial computer. God has reset the clock. Eden and everything in it is back to the beginning.

CHAPTER TWENTY THREE

With the collapse of the bicycle boom of the Gay 90s, the enormous profits raked in by Pope and others from their high-end machines becomes a thing of the past. Still, in America and England—and in fact, all over the world—inexpensive bicycles continue to be built. The machines now serve utilitarian purposes, as workmen ride to their job sites, businessmen to their offices and stores, children to their schools, and housewives to markets. Tradesmen use them to deliver their wares, and postmen, delivery boys, newsboys, and messengers use them to run their errands. In this new era the bicycle serves all those purposes admirably.

New enhancements continue to make the bicycle even more attractive, but the two most important additions were the free wheel and three-speed hub. The first allowed the wheels to turn while the pedals remained stationary, a distinct improvement in bicycling ease and comfort, since the rider no longer had to find a place to rest his feet while coasting. The three-speed internal hub offered three gears, with a lever mounted on the handlebars communicating with the rear hub via a steel cable. In the United States braking was achieved by back pedaling, and was an integral part of the free wheel mechanism. In the English system a lever mounted on the handlebars was attached to calipers at the rear wheel by means of another steel cable. Finally, with the addition of the seat tube, the structural member between the saddle and the bottom bracket, additional rigidity was added to the rig, and the diamond-shaped frame of Starley's Rover became the modern double triangle. Thus, the twentieth century dawned with the ready availability of a reasonably priced, reasonably safe, reasonably comfortable, self-propelled machine that was nearly ideal for covering moderate distances over varying terrain.

In England the leader of the bicycling industry for most of the century was the Raleigh Cycle Company of Nottingham, run by a cycle-loving lawyer, Frank Bowden. The company dominated the English market during the boom of the 1890s, and when that ended Bowden sought ways to put his business on a more even keel. In 1902 he retained Henry Sturmy and James Archer to develop a three-speed gearing device enclosed in the rear hub (three speeds were deemed to be perfectly adequate for all purposes). The result was the Sturmey-Archer hub, a much-needed addition to the bicycle. It offered a standard gearing equivalent to an ordinary's wheel of 60 inches in diameter, a lower gear for hills, and a higher one for down slopes, favorable wind conditions, and fast riding. The mechanism itself was fairly complicated, involving planetary gearing and many small parts that needed to be manufactured to close precision; but it was also rugged and dependable. It was completely enclosed in the rear hub, making it impervious to weather, an important consideration for a commuting and delivery machine. Raleigh and the three-speed hub dominated the gearing sector of the industry for the first half of the twentieth century, particularly in the commuting bicycle.

By the 1950s two styles of machines predominated in Europe and North America. The more up-scale version, championed by Raleigh, was a light-weight bicycle with thin tires, a three-speed hub, and rim brakes. The other, which appeared after the First World War, was a heavier but rugged one-speed model with coaster brakes and balloon tires. In Europe, Asia, and much of the third world, where the price of an automobile was beyond the means of the average workman, this bicycle was an intensely practical, cost-effective form of adult transportation. Most Americans, however, could afford cars, and preferred to ride in vehicles powered by an internal combustion machine. Consequently, the U. S. version of the balloon-tire bicycle was considered a child's toy. It was the so-called "kid's" bike or "newsboy's" bike, produced by a number of manufacturers, but closely associated with the Schwinn Bicycle Company, which introduced the balloon tire in 1933. These were heavy machines, sometimes weighing up to 60 pounds. To make them appear streamlined and progressive they were often given decorative elements reminiscent of motorcycles, automobiles, airplanes, locomotives, and rockets. Perhaps Schwinn's greatest contribution to the balloon-tire genre was the "Black Phantom," introduced in 1949. Sporting a streamlined tank mounted between double top tubes, chrome fenders, whitewall tires, headlight, tail light, horn and a shock-absorbing fork, the Phantom was the culmination of many a youngster's bicycle fantasy.

Both these models were replaced in the 50s and 60s by bicycles with derailleur gears. Like internal hub gearing, the derailleur was first developed around the turn of the century. The mechanism literally "de-railed" the chain from one sprocket and placed it on another; but for a long time it was no match for the more rugged Sturmy-Archer hub. The early development of the derailleur was undoubtedly hindered by the European racing community, which forbade its use for the first 30 years of the century, and it was not until the 1950s, when the Italian cyclist Tullio Campagnolo developed a means of moving the chain from sprocket to sprocket with a parallelogram device, that the modern derailleur came into existence. Various combinations of front and rear derailleurs were used, but the 10-speed conformation, with two sprockets on the chain wheel and five on the rear cluster, became the standard. This was the advent of the famous "10-speed bicycle" that came to rule both racing and commuting. Gears were identified by "inch" numbers corresponding to the diameter of the front wheel of the old high wheeler, and were calculated by multiplying the wheel diameter by the number of teeth on the front sprocket and dividing that by the number of teeth on the rear sprocket. A "normal" gear on a 10-speed was a 60 inch, meaning that with one revolution of the pedals the bicycle would travel as far as an ordinary with a 60-inch front wheel. A "granny" gear, or a low gear suitable for hill climbing, would be in the 22-26 inch range. A top gear could range from 98 to 110 inches.

Early versions of the derailleur were delicate. They went out of adjustment easily and required some degree of skill to manipulate. To keep cable lengths as short as possible, the friction-shift levers were mounted on the down tube, so that the rider was forced to take one hand off the handlebars (the right hand for the rear cogs and the left hand for the free wheel) and move it to somewhere around knee level to change gears. Once the chain had been shifted from one cog to another it needed to be adjusted, a maneuver effected more by hearing and feel than by sight, since an improperly centered chain would rattle or drop unexpectedly to another cog; worse, it could end up between cogs or slip off the chain rings entirely. But to bicycle racers and those who wished to emulate them, this and other drawbacks were minor. Since racers normally rode in the tuck position, with the back parallel to the ground and the hands grasping the drops of the turned-down handlebars, the position of the shift levers, only a few inches from the hands, did not present a problem. Furthermore, it was felt that the delicateness of the mechanism and the care with which it needed to be operated was a small price to pay for the additional gears it afforded. In an amusing replay of all the previous incarnations of the bicycle, the 10-speed derailleur racer found favor as an adult toy for young, athletically-inclined men; but what was originally a racing component quickly found its place on touring, recreational, and commuting machines.

In 1973 the Organization of Petroleum Exporting Countries, or OPEC, boosted oil prices dramatically. One of the results in the Western countries was a temporary shortage of gasoline and a spectacular rise in its price. Once again, the virtues of commuting to schools and places of business by bicycle became apparent, and the boom of the 80s was underway. The demand was greater than American bicycle manufacturers could fill, and many cyclists rode wheels imported from France, Italy, and Japan. The names of Motobécane, Peugeot, Bianchi, Fuji, and Miyata became commonplace. Competition was fierce, and before long a new round of improvements, such as indexed shifting, triple chain rings, and rear clusters with up to 10 sprockets, found their way to the non-racing bicycling world. At the same time a new phenomenon appeared, the mountain bike, designed by a group of Californians for the express purpose of careening down mountain paths. With its 26-inch wheels, wide, knobby tires, motorcycle-like brakes, a new frame geometry with a low center of gravity, thumb shifters mounted on flat handlebars, suspension systems, and "bullet-proof" components, the mountain bicycle and its more civilized city cousin, the all-terrain bike, swept the industry and dominated the market for years to come.

Nothing has yet replaced the chain-driven derailleur bicycle. With a clean and well-adjusted derailleur the chain drive transmits up to 98% of the rider's effort to the bicycle, making it one of the most effective energy transducers known. It is so efficient that in 1977 the chain drive was used to harness human power in the Gossamer Condor, the first successful man-powered flying device. That apparatus covered a course of 1.35 miles, but only two years later its successor, the Gossamer Albatross, flew across the English Channel, a distance of 22.2 miles. Both machines were essentially bicycles with wings.

CHAPTER TWENTY FOUR

"Then God said, 'Let us make man in our image, after our likeness. . . .' "So God created man in his own image, in the image of God he created him; male and female he created them." (Genesis 1:26, 27)

The noon-time sun sheds its rays on the clearing, but Adam and Even are not here. Adam and Eve are on the other side of Eden, wordlessly eating their midday manna. The snake is here, though, having slithered out of the underbrush only minutes ago. He has been summoned by God. He warms himself in the sun's rays for a bit, then calls out.

"God! God! It's me, snake. I'm here."

Out of the jungle strides God, in his guise as Adam. This time God-Adam is not wearing bicycle clothing, or shoes, or sunglasses. This time God-Adam is as buck naked as the Adam captaining the tandem on the other side of Eden. And God-Adam is steaming mad.

"This is all your fault, you wretched boa!"

"So you did it, huh? You pulled the plug on those two kids."

"Can you blame me? That pair of ungrateful louts! They rejected their God-given transportation. Sure, I know you gave them that *Celestial Bicycling Catalog*, but they deliberately chose to look at it. It was their choice to ask for those solo bikes. First shoes! Then helmets! Then clothes! Then sunglasses! Then water bottles! Then pancakes! *Pancakes*, for God's sake! Those pancakes cost me plenty! And now the solo bikes? No matter how many times I told them 'enough, do not ask for more,' they still asked for more."

The snake attempts to interject a comment, but God is too wound up to listen to him.

"No matter how often I increased the difficulty of their daily ride they still asked for more. I took away their tail wind. I took away their down-grade. I gave them heat, humidity, and hills. I threw everything at them. But did they ever figure out why things were getting so tough? No—they just toughened up themselves. They adapted! And it is your fault! You got them started!" God is plainly upset.

"Well, I don't blame you for getting mad," says the crafty boa, "but what did you expect? You gave them the ability to speak, so they spoke. You gave them the ability to learn, so they learned. You gave them the ability to think, so they thought. You gave them the ability to reason, so they reasoned. You gave them the ability to dream, so they dreamed. And you surely gave them the ability to improve their physical conditioning."

"Yes," thunders God-Adam, "I gave them those abilities but *they were not supposed to use them! Do you not understand?*"

"Sure God, sure, I understand, I understand. But you created them in your image, didn't you? You use *your* abilities, don't you? What made you think they wouldn't use *their* abilities—their *God-given* abilities? Just because you *hoped* they wouldn't? How were they supposed to know that? After all, you gave them free will. All they did was use it. You gotta be reasonable."

"I do not have to be reasonable! I am God!"

"OK, so you don't have to be reasonable and those two kids have to suffer for it, is that it?"

"No, that is not it!" snaps God-Adam. "Do they appear to be suffering to you? They are just back in their original state of innocence. And let me tell you, getting everything back to zero was not easy, even for an omnipotent. It was a lot of hard work and it just about wore me out!"

"Yeah, they're back in their original state, alright—back in ignorance, like animals. They have no idea who they are, what they are, where they are, or what they're doing. Is that how you want your children to be?"

God appears to be in deep thought. Finally, he responds to the question.

"Yes! No! I do not know! But I do know that this is all your fault. You made them speak, you made them understand, you have been giving them dreams, you have been urging them to ask for things, you have been making them covet bicycle paraphernalia."

"Well, yeah, that's true, but the pancakes and the solo bikes—those came from them, not me."

136

"Do not split hairs, you reptile. You know what I mean, and I know what you are up to. You've been poking Eve. Now you are trying to get them to discover intercourse. I do not intend for them to have intercourse! If they do there will be hell to pay. I will do this place in! And it will be on your shoulders!"

"My shoulders?" snivels the snake. "Why my shoulders? OK, I poked Eve, but only once. And OK, I admit I'm egging them on a little. But I'm not the one giving Adam those hard-ons. And when Eve sees his pecker standing at attention she really gets turned on. The poor schmucks don't have any idea what's happening to them."

"And they will not, either! Certainly not in the state they are in now."

"You're not really gonna leave them there, are you?"

"Yes, I am. That is the only way I can be sure they will obey my wishes."

"But here's the thing, God. Even if you leave them back at zero it's gonna start up all over again and it's gonna end up the same way. You created those kids in your image, which means you've given them abilities, and eventually they're gonna discover them and use them, whether I'm here or not."

"Yeah, well maybe not having you around would be the best thing. Sometimes I wish I had never created you!"

"Come on, God," reasons the snake. "We both know you could wipe me out in the blink of an eye if you wanted to. But you don't want to, do you!"

"Well I should! I created a perfect Eden. It was heaven on earth. And you ruined it."

"But look, God, when you created me you gave me that ability. Did you really think I wouldn't use it?"

"Yes, I gave you that ability, but that is *not* what I created you for!" roars God-Adam.

"Oh, I know what you created me for, and I know why you called me here. Those kids have really got you worked up. You're tense. You're on edge. You need a little relaxation."

"What do you know about relaxation?" sniffs God-Adam.

"Come on, God, you know I'm the expert. That's why you thought me up, wasn't it? That's why you created me, right? Even God gets lonely, doesn't he? This is why you called me here, isn't it? Just like the last time, after you created all this."

"Alright, I needed you then," admits God. "Creating this universe really took it out of me. Alright, I have those needs and yes, I created you to fulfill them. Maybe I should have chosen something other than a snake."

"Come on, God," cajoles the boa, "you know I did a great job."

"Well, I'll give you that," sighs God. "I did not think I would need you again, but I did not count on this disaster with that pair of humans."

"And now you do need me again."

"Yes, and right now."

"OK God, I'm ready for you. Go ahead, whenever you want."

"All right," replies God. "Just hold on."

With these words the boa's appearance begins to change. His vestigial limbs grow longer, his tail disappears, his body fills out and becomes upright, he grows breasts on his chest and hair on his head, and his scaly skin becomes soft and flesh colored. His features become human. Within seconds God has transformed the snake into a stunning Eve look-alike. Like God, she is buck naked. She approaches God-Adam, who enfolds her in his arms.

"OK, I get lonely," he sighs.

"See, that's the thing, God," says snake-Eve, eagerly returning his embrace. "Once you set these things in motion it's just about impossible to stop them. Like, how could it be only one time with us?"

God-Adam is gently caressing the body of snake-Eve who is responding in kind. "Listen," he says benignly, "you are only a snake, after all, so do not give me any more of your philosophy. That is not what I want from you right now. You know why I changed you into Eve. Do what you are supposed to do."

"OK, Big Fellow, no more philosophy," says snake-Eve. "Let's do what you created me for. Let's see what you can do with that celestial boner. But I have to warn you—this time it's gonna cost you."

A short while later, on the other side of Eden, Adam and Eve feel the earth shake beneath their feet. They see a spectacular display of lightning, with massive bolts of raw electricity shooting in all directions. It is a meteorological display never before seen in Eden, and it goes on for minutes, accompanied by distant crashing thunder and fierce, pouring rain. Then the sun comes out and all is calm again.

CHAPTER TWENTY FIVE

"Then the Lord God said, 'Behold, the man has become like one of us. . . .'"
(Genesis, 3:22)

As usual, Adam and Eve awake at first light. They have no recollection of having regressed to their original state, of Eden having been returned to its pristine newness. They have no recollection of once again riding their tandem at 25 miles per hour in a 100 gear in a cadence of 80 revolutions per minute, without speech, without toe clips, without shoes, without bicycling clothes, helmets, sunglasses, or water bottles. They do not recall that the macadam path once again sloped downward at two percent. They do not remember the 10-mile-per-hour tail wind that helped speed their pace. They do not recall that once again they ate only bland, tasteless manna three times a day. They did not bathe in the stream. They certainly did not regard each other as species members. Their memories of that episode have been wiped clean; in fact, that episode has been wiped clean from all of Eden. The last thing Adam and Eve remember is the terror they experienced when God appeared to be unleashing his terrible wrath on them. They remember his awful appearance, his dread-filled voice, his angry threats, his accusing finger, the heat of the flames that surrounded him, the way they pleaded on their knees, the thunder and lightning that accompanied his departure. They were certain that God was going to make them not exist any more. Instead, they awake to find that nothing appears to have happened to them. They see that God apparently has not punished them. Instead, miraculously, they see that God has fulfilled their request, because there, leaning against the walnut tree, they see two brand-new solo bicycles.

They run over to the machines, marveling at their beauty and grace. They are Trek 5000s, lovely wheels, bright blue, with white lettering and accent marks. One is larger and the other smaller, sized precisely for their respective leg lengths. The saddle and handlebar positions are exactly adjusted for their particular anatomies. Each machine has a triple chain ring and an eight-speed rear cluster. Indexed shifters are mounted in the brake levers. Brand-new plastic toe clips are attached to the pedals, and cages with water bottles are affixed to the down tubes. The bicycles gleam as the sunlight reflects off their glistening drive trains.

The pair are so excited they can scarcely bring themselves to eat their morning manna. They cannot wait to seat themselves on their new bicycles. Adam cannot wait to teach Eve the mysteries of indexed shifting. Eve cannot wait to experience the freedom of riding her own mount, doing her own steering, braking, and shifting.

Finally, manna eaten, personal matters taken care of, clothes, shoes, helmets, and sunglasses donned, water bottles filled, the excited pair mount their new wheels. What freedom! What joy! What pleasure! Yes, this is what they've been wanting all along, there's no doubt about it. Eve proves herself to be an apt student, quickly learning how to steer, shift, and brake. She conquers drinking from her water bottle while steering with one hand with aplomb. After the tedium of the tandem's friction shifters on the down tube, Adam is delighted with shifting his indexed gears from the brake levers. Before long the pair are cycling side by side on the macadam, chatting away. Riding like this is fun! But after a while they start to wonder. They wonder why God would give them these marvelous bicycles when he was so displeased with their request. They wonder how they managed to escape non-existence when God was so furious at them. And they wonder why God would even *want* to deny them these wondrous machines, when they explained to him that they were needed to satisfy their mysterious desires. Certainly, they reason, if God created them, God should know about those desires. He should understand them. But once again, they conclude, God's ways are mysterious and cannot be explained.

The lion watches them go by, puzzled at this new twist in his world. Adam and Eve are supposed to be riding a tandem, not solo bikes. There are supposed to be one set of wheels, not two. They are supposed to be riding one behind the other, not chatting and laughing side by side. The lion is not pleased by this disruption to his environment. He does not like change. He considers taking action, but the cyclists are gone before he can rouse himself to go after them. Besides, he has a meal in front of him that requires his attention, a freshly killed gazelle.

Before long Adam and Eve begin to realize that Eden's environment has changed again, and as usual, the change is for the worse. The macadam now appears to be cracked in many places, exposing the underlying stone. The uneven surface makes steering difficult and riding uncomfortable. The hills that appear before them are longer and steeper than anything they have seen before. Even with their granny gears the climbs are laborious. They reach the summits gasping for air, grateful for the rapid and dizzying coast down the other side; but each hill is followed by another, and another, and another. By the time they stop for their midday meal their legs are burning from the strenuous workout. The strain of keeping their machines steady over the exposed rock of the broken-up macadam has taken its toll on their aching arms and shoulders, and despite the padding built into their shorts, their rears are sore from the pounding of the exposed rock.

Their afternoon ride is even worse, with a vicious head wind impeding their progress. Shortly before they reach their final destination they are beset by a nasty cold rain that stings their flesh and chills them to the bone. Finally they arrive at their clearing, not realizing that yet another hour has been added to their day's circumnavigation. Riding solo bikes was supposed to be fun, but this is not fun! No wonder God gave them these bicycles—he did it so he could torture them. Riding solo bikes may be what was needed to quench those strange feelings, but they are paying a price for the privilege. Why is God doing this to them? As usual, they have no answers. They accept their evening pancakes with gratitude and exhausted, tumble into dreamless sleep.

Toward morning the snake crawls into the clearing, his eyes alight with anticipation. He parks himself near Adam, waiting for the youth to have an erection. Like Jack, the bicycling companion he met in his dream, and like almost all the other men on the RAGBRAI ride, Adam experiences three to five erections every night, as he sleeps. On occasion many of Adam's fellow RAGBRAI riders will awaken with a still-erect penis, but as yet, Adam's member has been flaccid at first light; hence, he has not been aware that this penile workout takes place during his slumber. The phenomenon occurs during periods of rapid eye movement, which is what the snake is looking for, and he does not have long to wait. Sleeping on his back, Adam stirs and his eyes begin to flutter beneath their closed lids. As if on cue, his penis stiffens. It is nearly time to wake up, and this will be his last erection of the night.

The snake slithers over to the sleeping Eve, who is pressed up against Adam. With practiced ease his prehensile tail goes to work on her nipples, bringing them to an erectile state. Eve stirs uneasily, her breathing growing shallow. The tail descends to her clitoris, delicately massaging that organ to tumescence. Eve groans in her sleep. She begins to breathe more rapidly, her skin flushing. Now the tail enters her moist vagina, and the aroused Eve is about to awaken. The snake quickly withdraws his tail and glides behind a bush to watch.

Stimulated by the reptile's tail and by the appearance of the morning sun, now just peeking over the horizon, the disturbed Eve comes to consciousness. She glances over at Adam, still deep in sleep, and is startled to see his penis standing erect and stiff. She has never been this close to one of his erections, and is fascinated by its length and rigor. What sort of strange thing is this penis, that changes its size and shape so remarkably, and why does it have such an odd effect on her? The sight of it is affecting her right now. Her nipples ache from distension. Her clitoris is throbbing. Her vagina is damp. A flush has overtaken her entire body. She is having trouble breathing. She has that unknown desire, and she has it bad. She rolls over, consumed with curiosity. Gently, she takes Adam's penis in her hand.

"Hungth!" Adam is instantly wide awake. "What are you doing with my penis, Eve? Did you make it get hard like that?"

Eve lets go. "No, Adam, I woke up and saw it pointing straight up. I was curious, that's all. I'd never been so close to it before when it was

143

hard like that. I just wanted to touch it. I'm sorry."

"*No!* I mean, *yes!* I mean, don't let go of it! *Hungth!*" Eve puts her fingers back around his penis.

"Hold it a little tighter. *Hungth.*"

Eve doesn't understand why Adam wants her to hold his penis, she doesn't understand why he wants her to tighten her grip, and she doesn't understand why he is making those strange sounds. But she is willing to oblige. Holding Adam's penis feels good, although her body is aching with that unknown desire.

"I think the snake had his tail in my vagina again last night," she reports to Adam, leaning on her elbow, her head propped up on her unoccupied hand, her thumb idly caressing his foreskin. "No, maybe it was this morning, just before I woke up, because when I did wake up I had that feeling that we get—you know, when we want something but we don't know what it is. I still have it. Come to think of it, your penis looks a little like the snake's tail. I don't know why I never noticed that before."

Adam has no reply. All his attention has been diverted to his phallus, now throbbing and quivering as if it had a life of its own. Drops of slippery fluid escape from its tiny lips. Gently squeezing the tip of Adam's penis, Eve continues her dreamy monologue.

"You know, even though I don't like it when the snake does that to me, it does feel good—it really feels wonderful. Maybe it would feel good if you put your penis in my vagina, like he does with his tail."

Again, Adam has no reply. His penis in Eve's vagina is a new concept to him, and right now he is in no position to deal with new concepts. Eve continues her gentle massage, her hand now lubricated by Adam's precoital emissions.

"Would you do that Adam? Would you put your penis in my vagina? I think that would really feel good. You could make it go in and out, just like the snake does with his tail. It may be just the thing we need to satisfy that feeling. The solo bicycles certainly aren't doing it."

Again, Adam does not answer. His brain has disengaged from his body. His consciousness is centered in his now painfully stiff penis,

144

encompassed by Eve's hand.

Eve is becoming impatient. Why doesn't Adam do as she asks? Why doesn't he at least answer her? Her body aches to have his penis in her vagina, but it's clear that it is not going to happen as long as she's holding it. Eve removes her hand.

"Don't let go!" pants Adam. "Why did you let go?"

"Come on, Adam," she pleads, her voice now husky, "I just want you to put your hard penis in my vagina, like the snake does with his tail. Please, Adam, I really want you to do it."

Eve's words finally register with her companion. He is grudgingly willing to oblige, although he can't imagine that his penis would feel any better in Eve's vagina than it does encircled by her soft hand. Not without a struggle, Adam attempts to figure out how he can fulfill her wish.

"OK, but how am I gonna do that?" he asks hoarsely?

"I'll lie down on my back and spread my legs apart. You can get on top of me and put your penis into my vagina."

This seems silly to Adam, but he figures that fulfilling Eve's wish is the only way he's going to get her hand around his penis again. Eve lies down and Adam awkwardly assumes a position on top of her, supporting himself on his elbows. It takes them a while to get things lined up, but eventually Adam's penis slides into Eve's genital canal. Adam immediately changes his mind. Eve's vagina around his penis is even better than her hand. Much better. Eve's vagina around his penis is better than anything in the whole world.

"Oh, Adam, that really feels good. It feels better than when the snake does it. It feels wonderful. I don't ever want you to take your penis out of my vagina."

Adam is willing to oblige. He wants his penis to stay in Eve's vagina forever. His entire body is quivering now. Adam has been reduced to a mass of jelly.

"Now go in and out, in and out, like the snake does with his tail," suggests Eve in a choked voice.

Clumsily, Adam begins to move his engorged penis back and forth as

Eve's hips rise to meet him. Within a few seconds the muscles around his penis contract and he experiences a violent orgasm. Eve feels his body shudder and tremble as wave after wave of his seminal fluid bathes her vagina. Adam is beside himself.

"*Hungth! Hungth! Hungth! Hungth!* Eve, Eve, that was it! That's what we wanted all this time! That was it! *Hungth! Hungth!* It was great! It was unbelievable! Did you feel it?"

"No," says the disappointed Eve hoarsely, "I felt something, but I still have that desire. I want you to keep going in and out."

Adam slides his semi-tumescent penis around and immediately achieves another erection. Again, he begins his back and forth motion, this time a little more skillfully. "This feels even better," he thinks. "I could do this all day!" And with that thought Adam experiences another climax.

All of Eve's attention is fixed on her engorged clitoris and her slippery vagina, now overflowing with their commingled fluids. Adam's ministrations are taking her to a brink, to the edge of a cliff. She has never experienced anything like this, certainly not when the snake's tail was in her. It's so pleasurable that it's almost painful, and Eve doesn't know if she can stand it any longer. She is thinking, "Should I tell Adam to stop?" No. She doesn't want Adam to stop. She wants Adam to keep going and going and going. Besides, every time his body stiffens and shudders, every time he cries *"Hungth!"* and every time his penis shrinks and grows again, she gets more excited. Now Eve is at a point where she is certain she cannot do this any longer. "Something is happening," she thinks with wonder. Her muscles begin to contract. Her body becomes rigid. Her sphincters tighten. Suddenly, with a glorious feeling of release, wave after wave of supreme pleasure wracks her body.

"Adam, Adam!" she sobs, shuddering uncontrollably. "You're right! That was it! It's marvelous! That's what we wanted, just like you said! It wasn't solo bikes at all. It's—it's INTERCOURSE!"

Adam is glad that Eve has found it, and glad she has named it, but he is not yet ready to stop. Neither is Eve, who is well behind her partner in occurrences of this delightfully fulfilling new experience. Finally, their bodies spent, their desires gratified, the pair disengage. An agreeable lassitude overcomes them. There is no thought of manna, no thought of preparing for the day's circumnavigation, no thought of their God-assigned obligations, no thought of the consequences of not fulfilling them. They fall asleep, their arms entwined around each other. They do not see the snake, his forked tongue flailing in and out between his thin lips, his tail drumming the ground uncontrollably, the tears springing from his eyes, the little red horns prominent on his forehead. He is rolling on his back, his silly little feet waving in the air, barely able to catch his breath, his body writhing uncontrollably. He is cackling with unbridled laughter.

CHAPTER TWENTY SIX

"... *therefore the Lord God sent him forth from the garden of Eden*.... *(Genesis 3:22)*

The sun is nearly overhead. The snake scurries into the clearing, his beady eyes shining in triumph, a grimace on his thin lips, his forked tongue fluttering in and out at blinding speed. He calls to the sleeping pair.

"Hey kids! Up! Get up! It's happening! You have to get out!"

Adam and Eve, their bodies still intertwined, languidly open their eyes.

"*What* is happening?" asks Adam, his brain still addled by the rapturous intercourse of only a few hours ago.

"The end is happening, that's what! God pulled the plug! I really, really didn't think he was gonna do it, but he did! This place is going down, and I mean down! You have to get out!" he repeats, his eyes shining, his diamond patterns glittering, his tail thrumming the ground, the little horns on his forehead glowing a dark red.

The snake's words penetrate their brains and freeze their blood. They separate from each other in haste, all thoughts of past and future intercourse driven from their minds.

"What are you talking about?" asks Eve with a shudder. "You mean God is going to make us not exist any more?"

"No, one way or another you're gonna exist, but no matter how, you're not gonna like it. The Big Guy is destroying Eden. You did it—both of you. This time you really made him mad! Get out or you'll die," the snake pronounces, as triumphantly as his thin voice will allow.

"Why? What did we do to make him mad? We didn't ask him for anything." asks the clueless Adam.

"Do? *Do?* What did you *do?*" repeats the joyful boa. "For starters, you *didn't* do your ride around Eden today. That's your contract with God. He created you. He gave you life. He gives you food and water. He gives you the bicycles. All he asks you to do in return is ride around Eden every day.

148

So what did you do this morning? You just went back to sleep. You ignored your obligations."

"Is that why he's going to destroy Eden?" gasps Eve.

"No, no, not that alone. That pissed him off, but he could have forgiven you for that. What *really* has his shorts in a knot is that you and Adam had intercourse. That was bad! You shouldn't have done that. Oh, my, is he mad! This time you really did it! I've never *seen* him so angry!"

"But—but," sputters Adam, "that was what we needed. Intercourse is what we both needed to satisfy those feelings we had. It was wonderful. It was the best thing in the world! Why would that make God mad? God never said we shouldn't have intercourse."

"Yeah, yeah, glad you enjoyed it. But you weren't *supposed* to do it and now you're gonna pay for it."

"What do you mean, we weren't *supposed* to do it?" asks the indignant and equally clueless Eve. "If we weren't *supposed* to do it why didn't God *tell* us not to do it?"

"Well," hisses the snake happily, "you know God. You never know what he wants."

Adam and Eve are oblivious to the snake's jubilant mood. Instead, their attention is focused on a far-off, deep, ominous rumbling that fills their ears. The ground begins to quake beneath their feet. The sky is slowly turning blood red, and they realize that frightening changes are occurring in Eden. Suddenly, with a blinding flash, a distant volcano errupts, spewing an awe-inspiring combination of red-hot magma, rock, dirt, dust, and steam into the upper reaches of the atmosphere. Moments later they are nearly taken off their feet by the shock wave and the roar of the blast. The mephitic scent of sulphur dioxide reaches their nostrils. The air turns chilly, as a cold breeze begins to blow. The rumbling and shaking increase in intensity.

Adam and Eve are now thoroughly alarmed. Despite the snake's assurance, they are convinced that God is going to make them not exist, or maybe even kill them dead, like the lion killed the gazelle. They are trembling from fear and cold, as the dry, chilled wind surges past their bare skin. The paper plates, cardboard boxes, and other waste they have carelessly been throwing into the underbrush are picked up by the rushing air and sent pinwheeling over the landscape, adhering to tree trunks and becoming entangled in branches. They accept the snake's easy explanation for the end of their world: they were supposed to ride their bicycles around Eden, and when they didn't do it they disappointed God. They had intercourse and they should not have done it because God didn't want them to do it, even though God never said so. Even if they had given the situation a lot of thought they would not have understood why that innocent act of supreme pleasure, why that rapturous coupling, why that deed that finally satisfied their unknown desires, should be something that would upset God. They have never understood God and his actions before, so why should this be different? But they have no time for thought. The quaking of the ground increases and the rumbling gets louder. The cold breeze increases to a gale-force wind, uprooting vegetation, bending branches and stripping leaves off trees, sending the captured trash spinning off into the distance like emancipated childrens' kites. Now they hear another sound: the wild cacophony of Eden's animal population, roaring, spitting, hissing, barking, trumpeting, twittering, clamoring, and bellowing in fright and despair.

"What do we do?" they ask the snake, shouting to be heard above the pandemonium.

"Get out! Get out!" he repeats.

"But how do we get out?"

"On your bicycles. That's the only way."

"But we can't get out that way. The macadam just goes around Eden. Around and around. It doesn't go anywhere else."

"It does now. Get on those bikes and ride out of here as fast as you can. *Now!*"

"But we have to put on our bicycling clothes first."

"No time for that."

"We haven't had our morning manna yet."

"Don't you kids understand me? I'm telling you, you have to leave

150

now. This instant! It's your manna or your lives!"

Petrified with fear, Adam and Eve leap on their bicycles and pedal away as hard as they can, while the snake collapses in a paroxysm of cackling, gleeful hilarity. But the boa has told the truth. The macadam path no longer curves around Eden; it now describes a straight path, leading to a dim, distant, unknown horizon. The noise of Eden's destruction grows louder behind them, the animals' shrieks unbearable. Pedaling desperately, their legs screaming in pain, their breath coming in agonized gasps, the pair come at last to the end of the macadam. A terrible explosion jolts them to a standstill. They turn, just in time to see the Garden sink into the earth and disappear. They hear one final desperate cry from the animal life, then all that is left is a foul cloud of reddish smoke and the faint echo of the snake's demonic laughter. The only home they have ever known is gone, and they have no idea where they are heading or what will become of them. All because of a little intercourse? "Why God, why?" they think. "What was so bad about that?" Yes, they were right all along. There is no understanding God.

Downcast, thoroughly chastened, the pair continue on their unknowable journey. The macadam path now turns to stone and rock. With heavy hearts they guide their bicycles over the bumpy, uncomfortable trail. Stone gradually gives way to dirt, then, after a while, to sand. Finally, thoroughly bewildered, the pair dismount. They drop to the ground with fatigue. They look around, their hearts sinking even further. They are on the edge of a desert. There is no longer a path to guide them. There is nothing but sand, as far as the eye can see. This is nothing like their verdant Eden! For the first time in their young lives they are hungry; but there is no manna to give them sustenance, and they do not know how to live with the void in their stomachs. They are thirsty, thirstier than they have ever been, but there are no cool streams of flowing water to slake their craving. Their bodies ache from their wild ride out of Eden, but there is no soft grass to ease their pain. They are disconsolate, the pleasure of the early morning's intercourse obliterated by the loss of their home and with it, everything they know. They do not know where they are,

151

they have no idea where they are going; still there is no recourse other than to press on. They remount their bicycles, but the wheels sink into the sand and the effort to make headway is too great. Sadly, they abandon the bright and shiny machines that only yesterday brought them so much joy. They proceed on foot, with the terrible sun beating down on their unprotected bodies. When the fiery orb finally sinks below the horizon, the fatigued pair lower themselves to the sand and fall into an exhausted and half-delirious sleep.

Rising at first light the following morning, their bodies stiff and sore, their tongues swollen, their mouths parched, their stomachs achingly empty, the bottoms of their feet blistered from the hot sand, Adam and Eve continue to wander in the desert, following the course of the cruel sun as it traverses the sky. For two more days they roam, their burned and dehydrated bodies bearing little resemblance to the god-like figures that yesterday ruled Eden. On the morning of the third day they see signs of vegetation ahead. They soon enter a jungle, a tropical rain forest, oppressive in its heat and humidity. After several hours of foraging they find a slow-moving stream of muddy, fetid water. They drop to their stomachs and scoop the warm, odiferous liquid into their mouths, drinking until they can drink no more. They search for food, but there is no manna here. As they rest their weak and exhausted bodies a large mongoose runs past them. Remembering the lion and the unfortunate gazelle, Adam lunges after the beast. Sensing danger the animal heads into the underbrush, but Adam manages to grab it by its long, furry tail. Ignoring the mongoose's pitiful screams, he marshals his remaining strength and smashes its small brown head against a large rock. The mongoose fights back, twisting its agile body and raking Adam's arms with its sharp claws; but Adam continues his assault until he has beaten the carcass to a bloody, hairy pulp. Satisfied that the poor creature is dead, he finds a sharp stone and uses it to dismember one of its slender forelegs. He samples a bite. The raw, sinewy, bloody flesh repulses him, but it is edible and he has no choice. He hands it to Eve and shears off another leg for himself. Adam has provided food, but he has killed for it.

Adam and Eve squat in the jungle, tearing at the raw meat with their teeth, the remains of the dead, mutilated mongoose at their feet. The blood runs off their chins. Their bodies are scorched from the sun, their skin is scratched and bruised, and their hair is hanging in tangled knots. Their once handsome features have become coarse; their once proud, erect bearings have given way to a slouching shamble; their bodies, once glowing with health and vitality, have shrunken to dull husks. Adam's arms bear deep wounds from the mongoose's sharp claws, and his face shows a four-day growth of beard. Eve's eyes, once filled with life and energy, glow dully, receded back into her head. This is not the benign, pristine temperate jungle of Eden, populated by healthy, satisfied, friendly animals with no natural enemies. This jungle is stifling hot, overpoweringly humid, and very dangerous. In this jungle the water is foul and makes them sick to their stomachs. In this jungle the underbrush, the tree branches, the thorny shrubs, tear at their flesh, and vines hanging from trees threaten to ensnare them at every step. In this jungle their bare feet are assaulted by exposed roots, sharp rocks, and crawling, stinging creatures. In this jungle hostile plants and insects attack their tender skin, raising large welts. In this jungle the animals kill each other for food, and the fetid stench of blood is constantly in the air.

The one-time inhabitants of Eden, the lords of the Garden, have started a new life. Before long their bicycles will be forgotten. The memories of their very lives in Eden will fade. Their memories of God and the snake will disappear into the distant past. Their memories of cool water from running streams, their memories of manna, their memories of the delicious taste of pancakes, will die away, and they will cease to wonder why they are being punished in this way. Living will be cruelly difficult in this jungle. After a while they will discover some edible fruits, berries, and plants, but these will not be sufficient to sustain them. To stay alive animals must be pursued, killed, and eaten. They will become hunters, because that is their only alternative to starvation. Their lives will be in constant danger and they will live in continual fear, as other, larger carnivores look for opportunities to feast on them. Now and again, when their brutish existence allows it, they will indulge in intercourse, although never again will they experience the innocent ecstasy of their first coupling. But Adam and Eve and their descendents will live.

CHAPTER TWENTY SEVEN

". . .you are dust, and to dust you shall return." (Genesis 3:19)

The sky is blue—a deep blue. I see some cirrus clouds, way high in the upper atmosphere, scarcely visible. "Why is the sky blue?" I wonder, as I fly through the air. Funny, that I should think of a question like that when I'm about to die. I even search back to the memory of a physics class and remember: it's due to a phenomenon called Rayleigh scattering, the fact that blue has a higher frequency in the visible electromagnetic spectrum, and it's the higher frequencies that are absorbed by the gas molecules of the atmosphere. The lower frequencies just pass right on through, while the blue color is radiated in all directions. The effect is named after its discoverer, Lord Rayleigh, the nineteenth-century British physicist. Fascinating, isn't it? You'd think I'd be wondering instead about why I got doored, why this is a bad one, why this is *the* bad one, why I'm going to be killed when I hit the pavement, because it's rush hour and the cars are rushing and that tan Buick Lucerne behind me isn't gonna be able to go around me or stop or even slow down enough to avoid hitting me, and even if he does I'm going high enough and fast enough so that there's no chance of my surviving this one. I'm gonna go splat. You'd think I'd be cursing that Yellow Cab and that stupid woman, old enough to know better, who got out of the rear door on the driver's side, right in my path, without time for me to swerve or even slow down, as if either one would have done me a lot of good, what with the cars around me all careening down Fifth Avenue. You'd think I'd be fixated on Newton's First Law, that an object in motion, in this case my head, continues in the same direction until it meets some opposing force, in this case the road bed. I could also be calculating the effects of gravity and air resistance on my trajectory. But no, I'm thinking about the sky!

So maybe what I'm saying is that the sky is going to go on being blue, whether I'm here or not?

Or am I saying, if the sky is blue it's still daylight out, meaning that I'm still in the prime of my life and too young to die?

Or am I saying that some incorporeal part of me will head for that blue sky when it happens? That it will zip right through it and keep going until it reaches Heaven? I don't really know what I'm saying, but it sure as hell isn't that. I never believed there's a life after death, another existence on a higher, spiritual plane, where all our bodily ills are vanished, where we're united with our loved ones forever more, where all is sweetness and light, where we sit at God's feet. Somewhere in the beginning of the Bible it says we're made from dust and we're gonna return to dust. That's one thing the Bible got right! My return is happening a little sooner than I expected, but I'm about to return, nevertheless. That Lucerne is gonna make road kill out of me, and my helmet isn't gonna be much help.

As for meeting God, I don't believe there's some grey-bearded fatherly figure dressed in a white robe and sandals watching over me and every one of the more than six billion people on this earth. And if that's what he's doing, he's doing a piss-poor job—a really downright terrible piss-poor job, with at least 90 percent of the population of this earth living wretched, miserable existences. Why does he continue to put those poor slobs here if all they're gonna do is lead such brutish lives? Is he some kind of sadist? I suppose those poor slobs are fortunate in that for most of them the wretchedness ends with an early death; but to attribute the quality of our lives to some all-seeing, all-knowing benevolent God takes the ability to hold a humongous cognitive dissonance, and I guess I just don't have what it takes. And people think that God has a plan for each of us? That God is a sports fan? That God is on our side in time of war? That God punishes evil and rewards good? That praying in church on Sunday is actually gonna accomplish something? Get real! We may owe our creation to God—and he may have paid attention to Adam and Eve and to a few generations after them, when there just weren't a lot of people—but as far as I can see he stopped worrying about our miserable individual lives a long, long time ago. Don't try to figure it out, because there's no understanding God.

Dying is tough, but for most people living is tougher. No wonder most religions promise such a happy afterlife. For most people, this one sucks. Most Americans—most people in the Western World—lead a pretty good life. Nearly all of those under the so-called poverty line usually have a bed to sleep in, furniture to sit on, a television set to watch, a car to drive, and food to eat. In most cases they have access to medical care, even if it is emergency room medicine. But for people outside those fortunate few, for most of those in the Third World, they don't get cars, they get starvation and disease; they don't get television sets, they go blind from ingesting parasites in infected water supplies. They're lucky if they get enough grain to subsist on, but the protein needed to sustain healthy growth is rare. How many of them have even a glimmer of the privileged lives we have? Not many, not many at all. Their lives are impossible, full of pain and suffering, and mercifully short. If this is God's plan, it's a piss-poor plan. It's not a plan, it's chaos.

Or maybe mankind is being punished because Adam and Eve ate that apple off the Tree of Knowledge. Well, I don't think much of a God who would punish thousands and thousands of generations for the supposed transgressions of two innocents. And anyway, if he didn't want them to eat the apple off the tree why did he put the damned tree there in the first place? Why did he give them the ability to learn if he didn't want them to learn? He was just setting those two poor bastards up for failure.

I always wondered—what about animals? Are we so superior to all life on earth that God watches over us, but not dogs? Not cats? Not lions, tigers, elephants, zebras? Not dolphins or whales? Not cows, sheep, pigs, goats, prairie dogs? You'd think the great apes would qualify—chimpanzees, gorillas, orangutans—they're so much like us. I read that we share something like 98 percent of our DNA with that portion of the animal kingdom. So does he watch over them? And what about the overwhelming proportion of the animal kingdom that aren't mammals? Birds, fish, lobsters, crabs? Snakes, lizards, alligators, turtles? How about insects: cockroaches, beetles, termites, flies, bees, wasps, ants, spiders? What about microorganisms: paramecia, bacteria, viruses, E-coli? They're all God's creatures, aren't they? Does he watch over all of them too, or are they all undeserving of his grace? Or is there a cutoff? Maybe he watches over animals that weigh more than 25 pounds? Or maybe he distinguishes watchability by the presence of an opposable thumb? Or by the size of the brain? Or by self-awareness? What about other living matter—trees, bushes, flowers, vegetables, fruit, grain—don't they deserve some consideration? Or is it as the Bible says, that all of it—the animals on the land, the fish in the sea, the birds in the sky, the stars, the very heavens themselves—it's all put here by God to serve man?

And suppose there *is* life on other planets; does God keep his eye on those creatures too? Would it depend on how man-like they are? And is he really the Lord of the *entire* universe? It's one hell of a big universe, you know, big beyond comprehension. Maybe he's just a local God, the Lord of our neighborhood—you know, our Milky Way galaxy, with its 400 billion stars and who the hell knows how many planets. Maybe there are other Gods who run the other 100 billion or so galaxies out there. And what if there are other universes? Ten of them? A billion of them? Five hundred trillion of them? Does he run them all? Maybe there's some Uber-God, a Diety who assigned our guy to create and run this little planet we call Earth. Or maybe God is more than that. And is he a he or a she or neither or both? Hell, I don't know—I have no idea. All I know is I'm gonna die, in just a few nano-seconds, and that's it. I hadn't figured this stuff out before, and right now I don't have the time. I don't have any time. This is the end for me, and God is not gonna save me. As far as my fate is concerned, God doesn't give a flaming shit!

They say that your life flashes before your eyes just before you die, but the only thing that's flashing before my eyes is the picture of that middle-aged woman getting out of the taxi. The way I'm pointed I can't see her, but I know she's back there, still exiting the cab, the dented door still open, my bike still smashed against it, her eyes still filled with horror as she watches me fly through the air, knowing that she's responsible for my death, but already starting to rationalize it. "It's his own fault," she'll reason. "If he hadn't been going so fast this would never have happened." Or, "Those bicycle messengers don't belong on the streets. It's their own fault when one gets injured or dies." Or, "Why does the city allow bicycles on these busy streets? Don't they know it's dangerous?" By the time she gets home she'll have it all figured out. Over dinner she'll tell her husband, "I saw a terrible accident today. A bicycle messenger got killed. It was his own fault for going too fast."

My fellow messengers will mourn my death. They'll come to my funeral. They'll wear black armbands for awhile. For awhile they'll say to each other, "Terrible, what happened to Adam, wasn't it?" But life will go on. I won't.

-The end-

SOURCES

The Bible, Revised Standard Edition. New York, Toronto, and Edinburgh: Thomas Nelson and Sons, 1952.

Fitzpatrick, Jim. *The Bicycle in Wartime: An illustrated History*. Washington and London: Brassey's Incorporated, 1998.

Wilson, David Gordon. *Bicycling Science*. Cambridge, Mass: The MIT Press, third edition, 2004.

Herlihy, David V. *Bicycle: The History*. New Haven and London: Yale University Press, 2004.

Cully, Travis Hugh. *The Immortal Class: Bike Messengers and the Cult of Human Power*. N.Y., N.Y.: Random House Trade Paperbacks, 2002.

Buchanan, Brenda J. "McAdam, John Loudon (1756–1836)." *Oxford Dictionary of National Biography*, Oxford University Press, 2004.

Made in the USA
Charleston, SC
28 May 2013